WINNING THE WITCH

Tori Ross

For the women who were persecuted centuries ago just for being a little different and daring to stand up to authority...and for the ones still being persecuted for the same reason.

CONTENTS

CHAPTER 1

Eliza

"What does this one do?" my best friend, Lily Jane, asks. She holds up a double-poured black and orange candle, sniffs it, and looks at me for an answer, her eyes wide like she's expecting a simple homemade candle to give her enemies herpes or make world peace.

"It smells good."

She places the candle back on the display table. "That's just plain boring, Eliza," she mutters, lifting another Halloween candle, smelling it, and haphazardly returning it to the sale table without thought to its proper placement.

"I'm sorry I'm not entertaining you," I chuckle, checking candle scents and colors off my inventory clipboard.

Lily Jane has been my best friend since third grade when my mother and I showed up at her house to help her mother with a small problem. Lily Jane and I were banished to the basement while the older women talked in hushed tones and looked through my mother's "house call" bag, as she called it.

Lily Jane showed me her Barbie camper that day, and that was that. I thought she was the cat's meow with her doll-sized pink camper, complete with slide and Ken doll without pants in the swimming pool. It was little girl heaven compared to the cauldron and spice bottles of dried frog parts I was given to play with. In return, she was happy that her father came home a week later after taking up with his mistress. We never really talked about it as adults, but we both know why my mother was called to her house that day, even if we didn't know as children.

My mother was the town witch. If you had a problem, she solved it. Did your husband run off with his mistress? He'll come home and even beg on his knees within one moon cycle. Did your sister take your half of the inheritance? Not to worry. She'll soon lose all of her money, and you'll gain your portion and then some. Bad skin? No problem for Lonnie Owl.

Our area was studied by the state university a few years ago because of the low invitro fertilization and fertility drug request rate in the county. They found no link to the high fertility and low sterility rate that they could explain. They were dumbfounded why women in our municipalities weren't seeking traditional fertility treatments when it's on the rise in every other county. Water was sampled. Power lines were inspected.

Then again, you can't explain that the town witch is on speed dial for half the women in the county. Most women were too shy to look at a scientist and explain that the local witch put a spell on her ovaries.

My mother died two years ago, unable to save her own life when her cancer hit. Many in town thought she was invincible and could never die. Unfortunately, that's a truth about my family's magic.

We can't use it for our own benefit. It's never worked that way.

"What are you doing tomorrow night?" Lily Jane asks, pulling me out of my thoughts of my mother. "Pouring candles that liven up the sex lives of everyone in town?" she asks, nodding to my storefront.

"Come on. You know I can't leave the house on Halloween. I'm lucky to open the door to children and give them candy. Even that scares the absolute crap out of me. I shove individual packages of Twizzlers into their bag and shut the door as fast as I can. I think it scares the kids, too. I have a feeling that I'm *that* house. You know, the one kids dare each other to go up to."

"Have you turned a child into a toad and didn't tell me?"

I laugh and roll my neck. "Not yet. But from the greenish looks on their faces when they ask for candy, they consider it an option."

"Haven't you learned how to control your issues yet? Your mom embraced Halloween. She walked around town with weights around her feet in homage to all your descendants being drowned as witches in Salem. She never had any problems."

I pull a box out from under the cash register and start stocking a nearby table with Christmas candles for the shoppers that will come the day after Halloween is over. "I'm sorry I can't control my power as well as my mother."

"That's what I don't understand," Lily Jane says, leaning against the nearby table and crossing her legs. She pulls her brown ponytail tight and tilts her head to the side. "Your power is controlled when you make your potions and candles," she says, gesturing around the room. "Why can't you control it otherwise?"

She's right. I've never been able to control my power except to focus it on the potions I make in my shop. As sad as it is to say, I became the town witch when my mom died. Except for some candles people can light to wish for a job promotion or to avert baldness, I've been the town disappointment ever since.

"I don't know," I grouse, not looking at her. "When I figure it out, I'll let you and everyone else that shows up at my doorstep wanting me to cure their husband's impotence or make their school board campaigns successful know. Until then, I'll just be over here in the corner, making my potions, melting them into the candles I make, and hating myself."

"I didn't mean to make you feel bad. Sorry," she mutters.

I wave off the apology. "It's fine. It's hard, you know? It's like if a father would have been a famous basketball player and got a son that couldn't walk and chew gum at the same time. Not only do I feel like I let down the entire town, I feel like I let down my mother. And she's not even here to judge me."

"You know she was proud of you."

"Was she? On top of that, I'm scared the town hates me."

"It's 2022. Do you really think people will chase a witch out of town with pitchforks and torches? Not only that, but if the town hated you, they wouldn't buy your candles. You do well here."

I blow out a breath that moves my hair as I stare at her for a moment. She's not wrong about my business. In fact, it's booming. Sure, most of that is on account that tourists like our quaint main street shopping area with homey ice cream stores, flower shops, and places that sell homemade soaps and bath bombs. The townspeople come in often enough, though, mostly around Christmas. Christmas candles account for twenty-five percent of my annual income. They also come when they desperately need something, ever hopeful that Lonnie Owl's daughter can do the same magic.

"Let's change the subject from my shitty witch abilities."

"Awesome," Lily Jane says, clapping her hands and smiling her grin that means she's up to something. "Want to help out the kids this year?" she asks.

"I always want to help out with the kids, but what did you have in mind?"

"You know how I was put in charge of the hospital's charity fundraiser and bonfire tomorrow night?"

"Yeah," I drawl. Lily Jane is a hospital administrator and tasked with things like charity events for the pediatric cancer ward. She's been planning the annual pediatric cancer research Halloween gala for months. "What's that have to do with me?" I ask.

"Well, we thought it would be fun to have a date raffle at the party."

"What's a date raffle?"

"You find women that want to volunteer for dates, kind of like a date auction. When guys come in, they buy a ticket for the date raffle. If the numbers on his ticket match yours, you pair up."

"That's both sexist and barbaric. I expected better from you," I snap. "And why do you keep saying 'you?'"

"How is it sexist?" she asks, furrowing her brow and ignoring my question. "It's volunteer. Nobody makes a woman offer a date as a raffle prize, and the winning numbers are matched randomly. It's no more sexist than that speed dating event we signed up for last year. It's not like a guy gets to decide or bid on which woman he wants like some sort of meat auction. It's just a spot of fun to liven up the night and meet new people."

I place the last candle on the table and break down the box, punching through the paper packing tape and folding the box down before winging it behind my sales counter. "Let me understand. A guy pays for the opportunity to win a date with a woman that he won't even find attractive. Let's not even talk about what the poor woman ends up with. She could end up with a creepy stalker or a guy that's nineteen and covered with pimples."

"The hypothetical woman could also win a date with a handsome billionaire."

"A handsome billionaire that has nothing better to do than to come to the small town of Rose Bluff, Ohio and take a gamble that his dollar raffle ticket will lead him to the woman of his dreams?" I ask, fake smiling.

"Technically, it's ten dollars per ticket."

"Are you actually asking me if I want to go out on a date with a guy that paid ten bucks on a raffle ticket to buy me?" I ask. "Because it sounds to me like any incel in the county can pay ten big ones and get some kind of date. How many basement dwellers are you expecting?"

She laughs and stares at me with her blue eyes with long lashes that I've always envied. My own lashes around my brown eyes need copious amounts of mascara before I leave the house or else people ask me why I look tired. "We're expecting around a hundred participants in the raffle, so we need a hundred women willing to volunteer for dates."

I catch a glimpse of myself in the mirror by the stockroom door. Medium brown hair in a simple bob cut frames my face. I guess I don't look so troll-like that I would disappoint a man that won me in the raffle. My figure is great for a twenty-eight-year-old body that thinks Doritos wrapped in pepperoni slices and dipped in ranch dressing is a balanced meal. Thank the goddess I like to ride my bike on weekends to stay healthy.

"What would I need to wear?" I ask, suddenly worried that I may not have anything in my closet. "Not that I'm sold on this yet."

Lily Jane perks up and straightens herself to a

standing position, jostling the candle table as she gets up. She claps her hands in a prayer-like pose. "You agree? That's wonderful! One lucky guy will adore you."

"Do you not hear words when I speak them?" I grumble. "Besides, not one male of this town has adored me yet."

"Now we just need to figure out what your costume will be."

"What the hell, Lily Jane? Not only does this have the possibility of being a dating disaster shitshow, but it's a costume party dating disaster shitshow?"

"Uh-huh," she nods. "Everyone will be dressed up, even people not in the raffle. We're expecting five hundred people to come just for the party. The bonfire afterward is open to the public. We're expecting kids there after they're done trick or treating if it doesn't go too late."

"That's a lot of people," I mutter, but Lily Jane ignores me. I tap my fingers against my counter and think about my costume options on such short notice.

"You have to go as a witch," Lily Jane says, reading my thoughts. "Remember that one Halloween that you dressed like a witch and handed out candy in the square? The town loved that!"

"That was five years ago, and I haven't left the

house on Halloween since. You remember what happened, don't you?"

Lily Jane grimaces, and heat moves up my own neck. I've spent a lot of years trying to forget the boiling coy pond next to the gazebo where I was handing out candy. Sure, most of the town doesn't *actually* believe the Owl family has powers unless they have some urgent affliction or situation. Then, they come to us, hoping for the best. But that night was an eye-opener for a lot of people. It was the night Eliza Owl boiled the pond water and killed all the fish.

I still have no idea why it happened. Stuff just happens on Halloween. It's the one night of the year when I have unlimited power, and I have no idea how to control it. I thanked my lucky stars it was only the fish that boiled. Imagine if I had cooked the children that visited the gazebo only because they wanted miniature Snickers bars from the witch lady.

Hence, the hiding on Halloween. The idea of going to a party with a thousand people in costumes scares the crap out of me. "What if I boil the punch?" I ask with a wry smile. "People already look at me like I'm a freak. Have you forgotten how they've treated me over the years? Egging my house when we were children moved to throwing rocks through our windows as teenagers. Do you remember the homecoming football game junior year? We had a bonfire afterward, and they chanted that they should burn me."

The memories of that night send a shiver up my spine. I ran all the way home at breakneck speed. Luckily, my mother told me to join the track team, probably remembering her own experiences running away from people hurling insults and whatever item they could find at her. The irony of a group of people hating me for being a witch and then secretly seeking out my mother's help wasn't lost on me. We never held it against anyone. People came to my mother desperate and broken.

Lily Jane waves her hand. "That was high school. If you boil the punch now, it'll only make the night more festive. Will you help me out or not? I need to find a few more women for this date auction or we're going to only be able to sell ninety-five raffle tickets."

"Five more women at ten dollars a ticket? You'll only be out fifty bucks."

"Fifty dollars can pay for a family's night at a local facility while their child undergoes treatment or provide crutches for a child in need," she deadpans, a prim smile on her face.

"Holy shit, you really just went there with the crutches. I mean, you didn't even soften that. You went right for the argument that denying a raffle date will make a kid lose out on necessary crutches."

"Are you in or out?"

I sigh and pull another box out from under the register, this one with Thanksgiving candles in rich browns, greens, and yellows, perfect to match the cloth napkins and tablecloths at the decadent turkey dinners. Maybe the idea of all of those families sitting around their tables, these candles the centerpiece, makes me nostalgic for family. Sometimes, I'd settle for just being invited somewhere socially. Not a lot of people want to hang out with the creepy witch that boils things. I can't remember the last time I was invited anywhere with a fish tank. Lily Jane is great, but she goes to Michigan to spend Thanksgiving with her parents. I'm tired of being alone all the time.

I'm especially tired of being alone on my favorite holiday, which happens to be tomorrow night. I have loved Halloween since I was a girl when I'd color paper witches for our door or color on our windows with glass markers. Mom would go all out on yard decorations and make the neighborhood children think they were at a real witch's home. Cauldrons that children could stir were placed on the lawn, and Mom would add inert ingredients and say spells that were really blessings before sending the children off with homemade popcorn balls and store-bought suckers. We'd also have a bonfire for the teenagers to roast marshmallows and surround at the end of the night, trading candy with each other. I didn't learn until later that only a few parents in town let their kids step foot in our yard. Mom would have entertained the entire town if she could have.

Tears well up in my eyes at the thought of what my mother would say about my isolation on this night. It was always the one night of the year when any woman in the Owl family can make just about anything happen. She'd admonish me for not using my gifts and hiding from my town like I'm a Salem witch from three centuries ago.

"Ok, Lily Jane. You win. I'll volunteer for a date. But if my date is nineteen with pimples or mentions living in his mother's basement, I'm out of there, and I don't care that you'll have to refund his ten bucks."

"Deal!" she says, extending her hand for me to shake.

CHAPTER 2

Jake

"When are you going to stop treating this place like your mother's basement?" I ask my roommate, Paul, kicking aside three beer cans before plopping onto our Ikea couch. I move a day-old pizza box and a fork to the side so I can put my feet on the coffee table. Paul sits on the other end of the couch, a bag of pretzels shoved in between his legs and a video game controller in his hand. "Did you work today?"

He grunts and clicks his controller a few more times before losing his game and taking another swig of beer. "I drove a few deliveries around at lunch. Foodie Ride isn't giving me my tips. I need something else when I'm not catering."

Part of me feels sorry for Paul and his lack of job prospects. Then again, in this economy, I feel like he's brought a lot of unhappiness on himself. He's quit eleven jobs in as many months and refuses to take anything but random catering gigs and run food deliveries to fill in the gaps.

It's not that I can judge someone for the bull

they have to put up with at a job. My job at the post office may have a great pension and federal benefits, but I happen to have a delivery route with a lot of stay-at-home moms that must be very lonely for male companionship. There are at least three of them that stand out at their mailbox and wait for me to deliver every day.

The unusual thing about that is that I see their handwriting in the return address area on the bills they leave inside their mailboxes for me to pick up. It's the exact same handwriting used to send themselves letters that they complain about not getting on time, using those letters as an excuse to stand by their mailboxes. I suspect they just want to come out and talk to me.

The other guys at the post office tease me about having every lonely woman in town after me, but I don't see it. Sure, I'm twenty-eight and worked as a male catalog model through college. I still have my full head of brown, tousled hair that I've always had even though some of my high school buddies are starting to thin on top. I used to wear glasses that skewed to the side anytime I played tennis, but I got Lasik a few years ago. Whatever it is, I'm now pushing thirty. You can't tell me the women think those tight blue pants that are postal service standard issue are attractive. I just see them as a one-way ticket to wedgie hell.

It's not like I'd even look at these women if they were naked, wrapped in cellophane, and standing in their driveway with a box of condoms and a tube of lube. I only have eyes for one woman in town.

Eliza Owl.

The first time I saw her was last year when I subbed for her regular carrier. Since then, I've crossed my fingers that her regular carrier will quit so I can ask my boss for the route that delivers mail to Eliza's candle shop. I arrive to work early every day just to see if her normal carrier is sick so I can pick up his route. Sadly, that man's healthy as a horse and never calls in sick.

"Get off my ass, man," Paul grunts, startling me out of my thoughts of Eliza and her rich dark hair and eyes I could get lost in. He runs his hands through his shaggy, unwashed hair and runs the hand down his stubbly jaw. "I have a catering job booked tomorrow."

I lean back against the couch and reach for a beer from the plastic cooler on the floor between us. Popping the top, I sigh and wish I could have a girl like Eliza. Kind. Beautiful. She must be smart because her business does well. It all combines into the triple threat of what I want in a woman. Too bad I can't figure out how to talk to her.

Every time I try to work up the testicles to visit her shop, I chicken out. I've never been particularly confident in myself, and the idea of walking into a woman's business and asking her on a date gives me hives. Literally. My hands sweat, and my lower back itches. When I get home and check the mirror, bright red dots cover my lower back.

"I'm working that kid hospital Halloween party tomorrow night. Want to go and hang out?" Paul asks, reaching under the couch and smiling when he finds a half-smoked blunt underneath the beige cushion. "Nice," he mutters.

"Sorry, man, but the idea of dressing up and going to one of those things isn't my thing. Besides, you'll be working."

"It's not a sit-down dinner event, so I won't have to worry about trays. I just need to watch the pans of mozzarella sticks and fried mushrooms and bring new appetizers out when those run low," he says. He takes a long drag off his joint and blows skunky smoke into the air. It lingers in the room, and I reach over to turn on the nearby oscillating fan we keep in here just for him.

"Still not my thing. Isn't it a costume party?"

He shrugs. "I guess so. I still have to wear my catering shit, though. Won't stop me from buying a raffle ticket for a date."

"A date? How are you getting a date with a raffle ticket?"

He takes another drag and holds it before blowing the smoke out this time. His eyes droop, and he coughs, pounding on his chest until he looks up at me like he's surprised to find me sitting in my own living room. "What?"

I pinch my nose and sigh. "You were saying something about a date raffle."

"Oh, yeah. I remember now. Yeah, dudes can buy a raffle ticket to go on a date with women volunteers. It's first come first serve, so I will definitely get a ticket since I'm there early. Hopefully, I'll be balls deep in my lady's throat by the time this thing is over."

I roll my eyes. Leave it to Paul to be disrespectful and expect a woman he wins through a raffle to blow him behind the dumpsters afterward. "What if you end up with a lady that doesn't...recognize your worth?" I'm not sure how to ask what happens if a woman doesn't want to service Paul after too much Halloween punch, but I don't want to hurt his feelings.

He waves the thought away. "I'm me," he says. If I suffer from too little confidence, Paul has a problem with too much. "Hey, you should come and buy a ticket."

"No way, man. I'm not spending money on a ticket so I can end up with some nineteen-year-old that lives in her mother's basement."

"What if the women are hot?" he asks, adjusting himself without any shame. "You could get lucky."

"With my luck, I'd get the basement dweller. Or

worse, someone like Millie," I say, shuddering at the thought of my ex-girlfriend. We broke up two years ago, and she still brings me muffin baskets every Saturday with little cards in them. I stopped answering the door a long time ago, so now she just leaves them on the porch, and I give the muffins to Paul. "No thank you."

"Hell, I'd love a date with Lily Jane Peters, but she's in charge of the event, so she's probably not participating in the raffle. Now that would be a hot little piece of..."

"What did you say?" I ask. My vision clouds, and my heart thumps in the vein at my temple as my brain warms up to a brilliant thought. I fist Paul's shirt, gripping it tightly as he looks down at my hand with a confused expression. "Lily Jane Peters?"

If it's the same Lily Jane, that's Eliza's best friend. I only know that because I see postcards come through the post office that are addressed to Eliza's shop. I may have looked at the sender's name once or twice as I was sorting mail, and I felt creepy doing it. I was just curious. They're all signed by the same woman that must get to travel a lot for her job. Lily Jane must be the woman that I see having brunch with Eliza on Sunday mornings at the breakfast place across the street from my favorite coffee shop. After I figured out where Eliza eats brunch, I make sure to always go get my cup of coffee and raspberry scone at the same time every Sunday morning, hoping I'll work up the nerve to "accidentally" bump into them as they leave. So far, I can't get my feet to move out of my coffee shop chair at the same time Eliza leaves the restaurant.

"What do you mean Lily Jane Peters is in charge of the event?"

Paul bites his lip and humps the air. "Someone else wants to tap that, huh? If you pay my share of the water bill, I'll let you share."

Why do I live with someone so absolutely disgusting? I shake my head like I'm clearing cobwebs from my brain. "No, I just know someone she knows. What did you mean?"

"Lily Jane is an administrator at Children's Hospital. She's the person that arranged the catering with my boss. I guess she's in charge."

"She'll be there," I mutter under my breath.

"Of course, she'll be there. She's in charge."

"Not her, moron," I say, standing up and chugging the last of my beer. I didn't even notice that I had almost finished it off.

I toss the beer into our overflowing recycle bin on the way to my room. Once in my own space, I breathe the fresh air not tainted with Paul's socks or old pizza boxes and quickly shut the door. I need to figure out what I'm going to wear to talk to Eliza. Hell, I have twenty-four hours to figure out what the heck I'm going to say to Eliza that won't sound fifty shades of crazy or peg me as a man that's read her friend's postcards and knows where she eats brunch.

I'm going to do it. Finally. I'm going to get some liquid courage into me tomorrow night and talk to the woman that I've been pining over for the better part of a year.

What if she's not there at all?

Surely, she'll be at an event her best friend is planning. I know there are a ton of rumors saying she's a real witch and can do magic, but I'm sure that's all hogwash, as my mother called it. There were rumors about a coy pond a few years back when I first moved here, but nobody really believes that. More than likely, something happened with the filtration system, and it heated that pond until the fish boiled. Even so, the rumors weren't helped by the fact that people say she doesn't leave her house on Halloween. Kids dare each other to visit her house, pushing the shy kid up to the front of the group and making them ring the doorbell.

Those stories and fears are ridiculous. Everyone knows magic isn't real. I mean, if witches are real, what's next? Werewolves? Vampires that sparkle?

I fling open my closet and groan. I'm a typical bachelor with uniform requirements at my federal job. I have a couple of suits for weddings or funerals and a metric ton of jeans and t-shirts.

What I don't have is a costume for tomorrow night.

I quickly pass over every shirt in my closet, swiping wire dry cleaning hangers to the side and trying to find something I can make into a costume. I could wear a flannel shirt and go as a farm boy, but that won't do. I need something more impressive. Maybe I could just wear jeans and a t-shirt, duct tape my standard box of Cocoa Puffs to my shirt, carry a knife, and go as a "cereal" killer.

I need something better. I need to look macho. Alpha. I need to look like a man that could walk up to a woman, grab her, and swing her over my shoulders before taking her to my cave to ravage her body as she moans with pleasure.

I pull out the black suit I wore to my Uncle Donald's funeral a couple of years ago. Inspecting it, I see a hot sauce stain from when Millie got mad that I wasn't talking to her at the buffet after the funeral and squirted hot sauce on my lapel. It was one of the numerous temper tantrums I endured of hers, and I scrape at the hot sauce, licking my finger to see if I can scrub it out.

There's no time for dry cleaning. I'll have to cover the stain. But with what?

I look on the racks above my closet and pull shoeboxes down, tossing them aside when I find them empty or not containing what I need. Finally, I find what I'm looking for in an old box that originally held hunting boots. As soon as I open the box, I pull out the paintball munitions holder that wraps across my chest like a bandolier.

I can go as a hunter wearing a suit. Do hunters wear suits? They probably did in the old days, at least. That's it! I'll go as a seventeenth-century hunter. The suit looks kind of old, like something an elderly priest would wear.

I need a hat. Something that will go with the outfit.

Scrambling to the door, I fling it open and walk back to the living room. "Do you have a hat?" I ask Paul.

He looks up at me with red eyes and crinkles his nose like he doesn't recognize me or that I smell bad. Maybe both. "Wha u ay?" he slurs.

"Do you have a hat?" I ask, speaking slowly like I'm a tourist in another country and yelling at someone for not speaking English.

He cocks his head and looks at the TV. "A hat? What the fuck do you need a hat for?"

"My costume."

"What are you going as?"

"I'm kind of throwing this together as I go along. I guess it could be some kind of hunter from the old days. I know!" I say, snapping my fingers. "What did they call those people that used to dress in all black suits and hunt turkeys for

Thanksgiving?"

"Pilgrims."

"That's it! I can be one of those guys. I mean, I don't think they wore bandoliers, but I have to cover this stupid hot sauce stain…"

"I have a top hat in my closet," he mumbles, pointing in the direction of his room.

I don't question how or why my stoner food delivery person of a roommate has a top hat, but I bolt to the room and open his closet. On the top shelf in the corner is a black, felt hat. I punch it a little to straighten it out and place it on my head.

I look in the full-length mirror on the back of Paul's closet door and admire myself. My pants tucked into boots would make my outfit look more seventeenth-century.

Hustling back to my room, I rummage through the gray storage tub that contains my shoes until I find the black Doc Marten boots I wore in college. I run my finger down the side of the still-shiny, black boots. Once I have the boots laced and tied, I look at myself in the mirror on my walk-in closet wall and nod. "I look like one bad Pilgrim mother fucker," I mutter, fingering the cartridge pouches across my chest. "This will have to do."

CHAPTER 3

Eliza

The overhead lights are off, and I hardly recognize the conference center ballroom without the harsh fluorescent lights that usually give me a migraine. The only other time I've been in this room is for the yearly public library book sale to raise money for funding the youth summer reading program. The place looks different when it's lit with only the orange and yellow Christmas lights that drape the walls.

Tea lights line the refreshment tables of appetizers, punch, and desserts. Bartenders in white dress shirts and bow ties offer beer and wine to early arrivals, and cocktail waitresses flit around the room with small wine glasses for sampling. Steam comes off the nearby pans of fried mushrooms, mozzarella sticks, and small pigs in a blanket. A man that looks stoned, complete with droopy eyes, rocks on his toes behind one of the tables. He meets my eyes for a moment, licks his lips, and winks at me before I quickly turn away.

"There you are!" Lily Jane says, wrapping me in a

hug from behind. "Complete with a perfect witch costume."

"You told me to dress as a witch, so I did what you asked," I say, spinning around as she holds the tips of my fingers so she can admire my costume.

I must say I outdid myself with my dress. It's basically just a jazzed-up, black cocktail dress. I didn't have anything too witchy, so I added a gray tulle skirt that I made last night. Lily Jane and I once made tutus for us to wear to a glow Zumba class, and I remembered that I had the leftover material.

I paired the outfit with the typical black witch's hat and even added a black piece of yarn with a spider ring attached to the end of it to hang down. As a finishing touch, I added some black chokers leftover from my high school goth phase along with some gray blush on my cheeks. It's really gray eyeshadow, but it works as blush in a pinch. I thought it added a little extra something to the costume.

Part of me is scared of how the town will react to seeing me in traditional witch garb. I'm hopeful they'll find it humorous that I'm simply dressing my part, and rock throwing won't be involved.

Lily Jane dressed like a Greek goddess. It's perfect for the event, and she didn't have to spend a lot of time and money on it with all of the other planning she had to do. A simple white sheet is draped over her and tied at her shoulder while a gold curtain tie cord dangles around her waist. For modesty, a white tank top strap sticks out of the sheet on the shoulder that's bare.

"You look magnificent," Lily Jane says, adjusting the knot at her shoulder as I stare at it. "You'll get a hundred dates, even if it's not from your raffle winner."

"I still can't believe I let you talk me into this."

"You'll have a great time. If your date is a dud, you can drink some punch, laugh at his bad jokes, shake his hand, and move on with your life."

"What if it's someone that already hates me? It's a small town. I can't imagine a guy will be happy to go out with me."

She looks me up and down. "If he doesn't appreciate you, you don't need him."

"Do you have good interest in the raffle?" I ask, looking at the crowd filtering in. Several men congregate at the raffle ticket table, handing over crinkled bills to the workers collecting the money or running cards through credit card readers.

"We're at eighty guys already, and the place is filling up. The bartenders are already getting tipped. This is going to be a great night. I can feel it. Absolutely nothing could possibly go wrong," she says, nodding at the band that's warming up their guitars and checking the microphone. "Even the band showed up. I'm marking that as a win."

My eyes flick to the raffle ticket table again and notice a man about my age. I only notice him because he's dressed like the stereotypical witch hunter my mother used to read stories to me about, pointing out their pictures as she turned the page.

Really? A witch hunter? Knowing my luck, I'll probably get stuck with him for the raffle.

Then again, as I inspect more than his costume, I realize the man is downright gorgeous. He has tousled hair that I want to run my hands through, and there's a dimple in his cheek as he smiles at the woman handing him change back from his twenty-dollar bill.

His shoulders are wide and masculine, and his teeth are white and perfect. Given that I was concerned about winning a date with someone that didn't have all their teeth, this man's presence is downright comforting. Not only that, but how cute would it be to have a witch and a witch hunter go on a date?

As a bonus, I don't recognize him. Is he visiting a friend from out of town or new? This is definitely not a guy that's toilet papered my lawn or slashed my tires.

The crowd files in, and the raffle ticket table closes up shop, selling out of the tickets before the event even starts. With Lily Jane busy, I look for a seat. I don't want to sit by myself, but I don't want to intrude on someone's party or ladies' night out. Squinting into the dim light, I notice the man in the witch-hunting suit. He's just settled at a table by himself and sipping a tumbler of amber liquid, whiskey perhaps. He looks around the crowd and smiles at people passing his table. From the look on his face, he probably wants someone to talk to.

I take a deep breath and steel myself for human interaction. It's no use coming to these things if I'm not willing to talk to people. He appears to be by himself, and he looks nice. Damn nice. He also didn't go to high school with me.

"Hi!" I yell, grimacing when I realize that I sound like a maniac. I didn't mean to yell. Why am I so damn awkward?

Startled by my voice, he spills his drink down the front of his pants as we both gasp at the widening stain covering his lap. He looks from me to his pants, then back to me, eyes wide and mouth moving like a fish as he searches for words.

"Oh, shit, I'm so sorry," I say, grabbing a heavy cloth napkin off the table and dabbing at his pants. I wipe in a circular motion as he raises his hands out of the way and stares at my forehead. "I think I can dab it here a little so that it'll at least look dry. Lucky you're wearing black, huh?"

When the circular motion doesn't work, I move the napkin back and forth with firm strokes as he sharply inhales into my hair. The napkin does very little to help the fact that his pants look like he's had a toddler-like incident, but I'm determined to clean his pants and make him happy.

I scrub and wipe, grabbing another nearby napkin when the original fabric becomes too wet. Unfortunately, he has another incident happening in his pants, and I'm making him a little *too* happy.

Dropping the napkin on top of his dick, I tilt my head to the side and grimace. I steal a quick glance at his face and find his stormy gray eyes hooded and dark. "Uh, Christ on a cracker. We have another situation. Um, I'll just let you take care of that," I say, pointing to his pants and grimacing at insinuating he should take care of his dick.

Why did I point at the erection I just gave the hot stranger after touching his penis? Heat moves up my neck to my face and ears, and the man covers himself with a napkin which really doesn't help. It looks like he's, quite literally, pitching a tent in his pants.

My eyes move to the emergency exit. If I leave now, maybe Lily Jane won't notice, and maybe this guy won't tell everyone at the party about the time the town witch jerked him off with a napkin at the charity Halloween party. Tears sting my eyes, and my forehead crinkles. "I'm so sorry," I whisper, waving my hands between us. "I was coming over to say hello because I'm here by myself, and you're here by yourself. I'm so unbelievably sorry for making you spill your drink and then being inappropriate about your boner," I prattle as he stays silent, staring at me. "Shit, now I've said the word 'boner,' so I'm going to go very far away from you," I say, pointing across the room. "Have a nice night. Hell, have a nice life."

He grabs my arm as I turn, but his hand isn't rough or unkind. "You're Eliza Owl," he says, his voice husky. Then again, it's probably husky because a random girl almost gave him a full handsy.

"How do you know my name?" I ask, the hard dick pointing at my belly button forgotten.

Great. Even the hot guy I tried to talk to has heard about my witch antics. I don't know why I could ever hope that the town won't gossip or tell awful stories about me to newcomers.

"Fuck!" he mutters, pinching his nose. "I'm sure I look really smooth here. I have a hard cock, and I look like I've pissed myself."

"All my fault, by the way."

"It's not. It's just that you startled me because I've wanted to introduce myself to you before, but I've never had the chance. I know you because I work at the post office, and I subbed for your regular carrier last year."

I inspect him closer, trying to recognize him.

"I'm sorry. I'm usually good with faces, but I don't remember seeing yours."

"You were counting money at the register when I dropped your mail off. Your part-time worker took the mail from me."

"Are you from here?"

"No," he answers, shaking his head. "I moved here after college because my grandmother lived here and was sick. I didn't go to high school here or anything."

"That's nice," I say, hoping to change the direction of the conversation from our near intimate moment. Maybe I can redeem myself. By some miracle of fate, he doesn't know I'm weird.

"How is your grandmother now?" I ask.

"Dead."

"Fuck," I whisper, looking around like a life-saving hole that I can crawl into will appear.

"Anyway, I'm Jake," he says, holding out his hand. "Let's just forget all this stuff happened, shall we?"

I shake his hand, and the warmth of his skin moves from my fingers to my wrist. His hands are masculine and strong, and the dimple appears on his cheek when he smiles at me.

"Eliza Owl."

He gestures to the seat next to him. "Have a seat

and tell me about yourself. Although, I feel like we're already close friends. Not everyone I meet gets me so excited."

I plop in the seat and put my face in my hands. My witch's hat flops forward, and he catches it for me before it slides off my head. Tentatively, he places it on the chair next to him before flagging down a waitress for another drink. "What would you like, Eliza?" he asks, the kindness in his voice too much for me to take.

"Arsenic."

"She'll have a white wine and a water," he orders.

I lift my head and peer at him from between my fingers. "How did you know I like white wine?"

He clears his throat. "Lucky guess since most of the women I've dated like white wine."

I nod and blow out a breath. I roll my neck and try to think of something to say that won't bring up his dead grandmother, his wet pants, or the fact that his dick felt absolutely gigantic under my fingers. Heat moves up my body at the thought of it.

"They say you're a real witch and that you boiled the coy pond."

"All true," I deadpan, not having the strength to lie.

He crinkles his nose and purses his lips. "You know, most people would deny that to a total stranger."

I wave around the ballroom. "This is my first Halloween out on the town in ages. There's a reason I don't leave the house. For one, most of the town hates me. Honestly, I'm exhausted of hiding, and I'm so frustrated that I do stupid shit on Halloween."

"Why is that?"

"Why am I frustrated?"

"That, and why do you do stupid shit on Halloween?"

The waitress brings over a glass of white wine and water for me and hands Jake another round of whatever I made him spill. The strong smell of it confirms the whiskey, and he takes a deep gulp before I answer him. He doesn't grimace at the taste or sip like an amateur. This is a man that knows his hard liquor and likes it.

He sets the glass on the table and leans back in his chair, crossing his legs and focusing on me. My heart thuds at his full attention, and I drop my hands to my lap. Maybe I can still redeem myself and have a lovely conversation with the guy dressed like a witch hunter.

Wait a second. Is he dressed like a witch hunter because he's a zealot or something? Maybe he really is against witches, and I just told him that I'm a witch. If the other town citizens got to him and warned him about me, he may be here to get me to like him before denigrating me and trying to cast out my demons. Is this a joke? Am I being set up in a middle school-type prank?

Then again, I approached him first. Surely, if it was a prank orchestrated by the town, he would have approached me.

Before I can answer him, the stoned man from the appetizer table approaches us and punches Jake's shoulder from behind, causing Jake to slosh his drink on his pants again. "Fuck!" Jake grunts.

"Sorry, man," the man drawls. He nods at me with a smirk and extends his hand. "Paul Arthur. That's my full name, not my first and middle. A lot of people think that."

I shake Paul's hand as Jake dabs at his pants again, the wet stain taking up half his entire lap now and dripping into the chair. Paul's hand is clammy, and the smell of skunk wafts off of him. Not only is he stoned, but he can't even smoke the good stuff.

"Yeah, Paul, this is Eliza. Eliza, this is my roommate, Paul."

"You in the raffle?" Paul asks, licking his lips.

"Uh, yeah. I assume you bought a ticket?"

"Sure did. Maybe we'll end up together. You. Me. Moonlight out back," he winks, jabbing his thumb over his shoulder at the fire exit that leads to the dumpsters. Jake rolls his eyes behind Paul.

"Sounds romantic," I mutter.

Paul turns to Jake and ruffles his hair. "I just came over to give you my date raffle ticket. I don't have any pockets in my pants, and I keep setting this down and forgetting where I left it. Can you put this in your pants?"

"Sure, whatever. Give it here," he says, putting Paul's ticket in his pocket. "Yours is in my left pocket. Mine is in my right."

"Got it, thanks," he says, turning to leave. "Nice to meet you, Lizzy. I hope I win you," he laughs.

"It's Eliza," I correct, but Paul's already halfway back to the appetizer table, stopping to pour something from a flask into a punch bowl.

"Sorry about him. I was lonely after Grandma died. I needed a roommate when I moved into her house. He's not a gentleman, that's for sure. For what it's worth, I hope you don't get paired with him. He pays rent and utilities and doesn't eat my food, but we're not best friends."

"If you don't like him, why don't you kick him out?"

He looks off into the distance like he's never thought of that before and adjusts the bandolier across his wide shoulders. "Have you looked at the town's eviction rules? Even if I could kick him out, it's more trouble than it's worth."

I put my elbows on the table and look closer at him. "You're awfully mature about a lot of things."

"I am?" he asks.

"You've had whiskey spilled on you twice, your roommate is a sexist imbecile, and I don't even want to talk about the napkin incident. Yet, you've not been flustered at all except for being shocked when I came over to talk to you. It's like...you're a real man."

He smiles a toothy smile and looks into my eyes before looking above my head. His eyes go wide, and he slides out of his chair, slinking down to the ground into a squat. "Holy shit!" he says, crawling under the table and grabbing onto my ankle so hard that I yelp. So much for maturity.

"What the hell is happening now?" I ask, looking from left to right for an intruder or man with a gun. I don't even see a scary costume. Most people are dressed like farmers for some reason. It must be an easy costume.

"Don't talk to her," he mutters, flipping up the tablecloth so I can look down and see his face. "Don't talk to her when she comes over. I think she spotted me. In fact, run if you can."

"Don't talk to whom?" I ask.

"My ex-girlfriend is here. Her name is Millie, and...holy shit," he says, pulling the tablecloth around his face again. He taps my knee just as I see a gorgeous woman of about thirty strolling toward my table, her head held high.

Of course, a woman this beautiful would date a guy as hot as Jake. She probably has some nice, normal job at an office and has never boiled living animals with faulty witchcraft.

She stops at my table, looking down the tip of her long nose at me and curling her upper lip. Her red hair is back in a bun, and she's wearing a naughty nurse costume paired with bright red lipstick. Red high heels cover her feet, and she taps them impatiently.

"Hi, I'm Eliza," I say, extending my hand to the woman. She bats it away with a large smack that hurts, and she snorts at me. "OK, we aren't shaking hands. That's cool. Not really much of a handshake person myself…"

"Jacob Salt," she interrupts. "You come out of there right this minute. I already saw you, so you can't hide. We have business to discuss, and I demand to know why you're here with this floozy."

CHAPTER 4

Jake

My erection was already going down, but Millie's voice makes my balls retract into my body, my dick shriveling to the size of a grape. What the hell is she doing here? More importantly, how could anyone call Eliza a floozy? My heart thumps that I have to deal with this, but heat rises to my face and ears at Millie calling the woman who is first place in my heart and my spank bank a floozy.

"Millie? What are you doing here?" I ask, sticking my head out from under the tablecloth and acting surprised to see her.

Eliza takes a deep breath, and both women look at me with creased brows. The difference between them is palpable, though. One is angry. The other is calm and watching with fascination like she's watching a baseball game.

"I'm here for the raffle," Millie screeches. "I have pined over you for two years since you dumped me, and I'm not going to wait around for you to come to your senses and beg for me to take you back. What the hell are you doing under the table?"

"I-uh," I stutter, my mouth dry and unable to move. "Well, Eliza told me her feet hurt, so I was just..." I straighten my suit as I pull myself back into my chair and take a quick drink of what's left of my whiskey. "I was massaging her feet," I say with the smoothest shrug I can muster.

Eliza covers her mouth, stifling a laugh. Millie, on the other hand, flushes and grits her teeth. "How dare you cat around town?"

"Millie, we broke up two years ago."

"I gave you everything!" she yells, jabbing her finger into my chest. Passing caterers gawk, and people at nearby tables turn around.

"Millie, do you remember this?" I ask, pulling my bandolier to the side and showing her the hot sauce stain on my lapel. "You had a temper tantrum and threw hot sauce on me at a funeral."

"You ignored me."

"It was a funeral, Millie. You weren't the star of the show. That's not how funerals work. The dead person and their family are usually the focus."

Millie pulls out the chair next to me and sits down, fluffing her naughty nurse skirt and batting her eyelashes at me. "Are you in the raffle?" she asks, changing the subject.

"Yeah," I drawl.

"I hope I win you," she says, sliding her hand up my thigh. When she reaches the spilled whiskey, she pulls her hands back. "Lord, did you pee yourself?"

"It's spilled whiskey," I mumble. "Millie, have you met Eliza?"

"No, and I don't care to meet your side piece trash," she says, smiling a mean grin.

Eliza, for her part, sips the last of her wine before she calmly sets down the glass and stands up from the table, smoothing the gray tulle around her skirt. "I'll leave you two to catch up," she says.

"Please stay. I'm begging you."

"It was nice to meet you, Jake," she says. "Good luck in the raffle, Millie."

As soon as she's out of earshot, I turn on Millie. "How dare you talk to a nice woman like that? She has more class in her middle finger than you have in your entire body. What the hell is wrong with you? We are done! We've been done for two years," I say, gritting my teeth and shaking with anger. Millie rears back like she wasn't expecting me to stick up for myself. "Stop leaving your damn muffins on my doorstep. They're dry, you add too much cinnamon, and I give them to my new roommate anyway."

She gasps and opens her mouth to speak, but we're interrupted by a tapping on the microphone at the front of the room. Lily Jane Peters adjusts the microphone and clears her throat. "Thank you all for coming," she says to applause.

Another couple comes to our table and sits down with us, and I scan the room for Eliza. Since Millie ruined our conversation, the room has quickly filled, and a crowd has formed near all of the appetizer tables and the bar. I can't find her. Did she leave?

"Before the band starts to play, we wanted to announce your raffle pairings. That way, you can enjoy the company of your date for the entire evening," Lily Jane explains.

"Or be in hell the whole night," I mutter under my breath. Under the table, Millie puts her hand on my leg and squeezes. I bat her hand away and listen as Lily Jane asks each couple to meet back at the raffle table to be paired with their date for the night.

I jostle my leg and move my eyes around the room as Millie drones on about her life in the last two years and Lily Jane calls out numbers. Men and women move around the room to meet at the raffle table, and I watch each pairing, worried about who will win a date with Eliza. When each number is called, I look at the tickets I've fished out of my pocket, Paul's on the left and mine on the right. Seventy and then eighty couples pair off, congregating around the room with wine glasses and appetizer plates as Lily Jane keeps calling numbers.

"If you have number 8675307, go to the raffle table."

Millie jumps up beside me. "That's me. What number did you get?" she asks, trying to catch a glimpse of one of the raffle tickets in my hand. I quickly cup my hands around the tickets until she gives up and walks away to meet her date.

As soon as she's gone, I peek at the ticket numbers and gasp when I see that the ticket in my right hand matches Millie's number. My vision tunnels, and a scream of terror lodges in my chest. I look at the back emergency exit and wonder how fast I can run to my car. Sweat drips behind my ear, and my stomach growls like I suddenly need to get to a toilet.

"Up next, if you have 8675308, go to the raffle table."

Another look at my ticket shows me that Paul's ticket in my left hand has that number. I need to tell him to go to the ticket area.

Out of the corner of my eye, I see gray tulle swish past the table. Eliza! She doesn't say hello or stop to talk. She marches straight to the raffle table and crosses her arms several feet away from Millie as they both wait for their dates to show up.

The realization that I'm holding the ticket to the woman of my dreams in my left hand muddles around in my brain. It's Paul's ticket, and there is no way that I'm going to let my misogynistic stoner of a roommate within two feet of Eliza. The idea hits me, and I do what any other man would do in my situation.

I get up from the table, and switch the tickets, putting Millie's ticket in my left pocket and Eliza's ticket in my right.

I'm going to show Eliza the best night of her life, and I'll do anything to make that happen.

"Hey, Paul," I say, cutting the line to the catering area and nonchalantly picking up a mozzarella stick. "Here's your raffle ticket."

"My what?"

I sigh and chew on the appetizer as I look over and see Eliza check the time on her phone while she waits for her raffle date to show up. She looks around with sad eyes, probably thinking nobody is coming for her. I can't let her feel like that a second longer. I'm desperate for her to know that she's wanted and that it's me that wants her.

"Your ticket, asshole. Here," I say, sliding it across the table through a small puddle of punch. "See you later."

I turn from Paul and march to the raffle table. Millie's face lights up as soon as she sees me approach, but I need to play this cool. I can't let the ladies know that I know who I'm here for.

I hold my ticket out to the event coordinator who matches my number on her clipboard. The woman smiles at me, even as I feel Millie's eyes on the back of my head. "Ticket 8675308? Ma'am, this is your raffle date winner for the evening," the woman says, gesturing to Eliza.

A sheepish grin crosses her face as I hold out my hand to her. "Let's start over."

"I'd like that," she says, shaking my outstretched hand. "Eliza Owl. Alleged pond boiler and candle shop owner," she says, smiling a genuine grin.

"Jake Salt. Postal service worker."

"Wrong! Nope. Nuh-uh," Millie yells behind me. When I turn around, she's waving her arms like she's swatting away flies. "You're mine, Jake Salt. Now and forever. Get used to it!"

She grits her teeth and balls her fists, and I step in front of Eliza, my arms outstretched, just in case Millie takes a punch at her. "Millie, turn your crazy off!" I yell back.

"What's going on?" Paul asks, handing his ticket to the woman at the table.

The woman must be used to maniacal outbreaks because she checks Paul's name off her list and points to Millie without any concern for the shit show in front of her. "This is your date, Mister Arthur."

"Nice!" Paul says, looking Millie up and down. "You're hot as fuck. You like backseats?"

"Fuck no! This is your roommate, isn't it, Jake?"

"What does that have anything to do with this? This is your raffle winner. I'm not in charge of the raffle, for fuck's sake."

Millie steps toward me until the tips of her high heels touch the end of my boots. "You switched the tickets somehow. I know you did. I call shenanigans!"

"I did no such thing," I lie, my teeth bared and lips tilted into a smile. "If you think I tampered with the system, by all means," I say, sweeping my hand toward the raffle table. "Prove it, Millie."

She looks from left to right, biting her lip. "I'm going to get you back, Jake. We'll be married if it's the last thing I do," she whispers.

"Can we all just calm down?" Eliza asks behind me. "It's a simple raffle date at a charity party. Nobody is running off to get married. Let's just step back and talk like adults."

I nod at what Eliza says, but Millie isn't having it. "Listen here. This man is mine, you cheap slut. Mine, I tell you! I worked hard for him and have tried to win him back for the last two years. I'm not about to let some basic bitch in a basic bitch costume come up here and…"

Silence fills the conference center entryway, and I back up from Millie in slow motion. Paul cocks his head to the side and examines Millie like he's not sure what he's seeing. Frankly, I'm not either. Looking around, nobody else notices anything different. The woman at the table is looking at her clipboard and directing people to their dates. The music plays in the ballroom behind me, and I also hear distant laughter and punch glasses clinking.

What I don't hear are the words Millie's screaming as her faces turns red a few inches from my nose. Her hands come to her throat, and I reach around to pat her back. Is she choking on something? I don't think she had anything in her mouth. Can you choke to death on your own spit?

Her eyes dart from me to Eliza, and she puts her hands on my shoulders, shaking me. "What's wrong? Do the universal choking sign if you need help, Millie."

She shakes her head and inhales deeply through her nose. She blows out the breath, so I know she can breathe, but she only hums. I remove her hands from my shoulders and stare at her.

"What do you think is wrong with my date?" Paul asks.

"I don't know. It's like she just stopped talking."

Paul looks at her a moment and sighs. "Think she can still use her mouth? If she can't swallow, that's going to put a damper on my..."

"Shut the fuck up!" I snap. "Something's wrong with her. Millie, listen to me." She shakes her head back and forth so quickly that I'm concerned she'll get whiplash. She pulls at her hair, and people passing by look at her funny as she moans. "Millie, open your mouth and let me see if something is wrong," I direct.

She does as I ask, tears trickling down her face, and I look inside her mouth. I see gums, her familiar teeth, and her uvula dangles at the back of her throat, but there's a disturbing absence at the bottom of her mouth. "Holy shit! Did you swallow your tongue?"

"What do you mean she swallowed her tongue?" Paul asks.

"It's not there. She has no tongue."

"Oh, shit," Eliza whispers behind me.

"Do you think I can trade my ticket in for a different date? This one can't lick my sack like I like," Paul says, and I grab his shirt, shaking him until he stops talking and his eyes roll.

"Oh, God," Eliza says again, covering her face with her hands. "I'm so sorry. I need to go."

I turn around and shake my head at Eliza, Millie's lost tongue forgotten. "Don't leave!"

Eliza backs away from me and heads to the door, pulling her purse over her head and knocking her hat sideways. "I'm sorry, Jake," she says, opening the door. "And I'm so sorry, Millie."

Millie grunts and cries in front of me as my dream woman runs out the door.

CHAPTER 5

Eliza

My black high heels clack against the old cobblestone brick as I run as fast as I can away from the Halloween party. Jake pushes both center doors open at the same time in a way I'd think is sexy if I hadn't just made his ex-girlfriend lose her tongue.

Literally.

This is worse than the coy pond. Not that fish don't have feelings, but I only boiled fish that time. This time, I hurt a human woman.

Granted, she's dreadful, and Lily Jane would probably tell me Millie deserved to have her tongue removed for the awful things she said to me and the way she talked to Jake like she owns him. I didn't mean to do it, though. I just wanted her to shut up. I wished it inside my head, and I didn't even have to mutter a spell or secretly wiggle my fingers under a table. I simply wanted her to shut the fuck up.

Then, when I realized what I'd done, I wanted to reverse it and couldn't. Maybe I'm too panicked right now to do the reversal. Spells for our own good don't always work just like my mom couldn't fix her cancer. Maybe, when I shut Millie up, that was for the good of Jake. Then, getting her voice back was for my own good to save my ass. Whatever the reason, I couldn't fix Millie.

Maybe I'm just broken. I have years of trauma under my belt. I've been called useless and sinful, and I've been told that I'm going to hell in a handbasket. Hearing myself called side piece trash and the way she talked to Jake...something just snapped.

"Eliza, wait!" Jake calls, his heavy witch hunter boots not far behind me. "Please come back! Tell me what happened."

I run faster until my heel gets caught in the sidewalk, and I fall face-first toward the pavement. My hands hit the concrete, and my knees scrape like they did when I would fall on walks with my mother as a child. A quick look down shows dark scrapes across both knees, a scuffed high heel, and dots of blood appearing on my hands and knees like pinpricks.

"Eliza, are you OK?" Jake asks, suddenly at my side and holding my leg. He pushes my tulle skirt up my thigh so he can see my leg, and I'm reminded of weddings when a man lifts his bride's leg up to find the garter.

"I'm fine, Jake. It's just some scrapes," I say,

pushing my skirt down and moving his hands away. It's hard to move them, though. They're firm and warm, and I very much want them on my leg. Chills move up and down my back at his touch, but I shouldn't be thinking about that right now.

"Why were you running from me? What happened?"

I shake my head. "I can't tell you. You'll hate me."

"Trust me when I say that I could never hate you."

I look into his eyes, and they're kind. Concern wrinkles his brow. "How can you say that? You don't know me. You don't know what I'm capable of," I snap, pushing myself off the concrete and grimacing at the sting in my palms as I lift myself.

He stands up with me, grabbing my hands and turning them to see the blood. "Eliza, I have a first aid kit in my car. Let's go get it. We can clean you up and talk about this."

"I just want to go home."

"You'll get blood all over your steering wheel. It'll just take a few minutes. It's right over here," he says, gesturing to the parking lot and pulling me toward it.

I let him lead me to a black convertible with beige leather seats and stand to the side as he opens the car door and rummages through his glove compartment. I flick my eyes in the direction of my own small sedan and think about running again. What if I hurt him?

"Let's see...I'm not sure how much I have and how old it is, but I should be good for some bandages, at the very least," he mumbles.

"This is a really nice car," I say. "Are you a secret billionaire who works as a letter carrier for fun?"

He chuckles and opens a plastic kit, holding up a small packet of antibiotic ointment to check the expiration. "I inherited some money, and my house was my grandmother's. I don't have a mortgage, so I wanted a hot car. I'm not a billionaire, though. Sorry if that disappoints you. Come here," he says, pushing his passenger seat forward and waving to the back seat.

"I don't know about getting in the back seat of a car with a stranger on the first date."

"Shit, you probably think I'm like Paul. At least the roof is open."

"True," I shrug, climbing into his car. "I guess you can't quietly murder me in an open convertible at a charity event."

"Sit up on the back of it if it makes you feel better. Someone passing by can see you."

"Like I'm in a parade?"

He smiles, and the sexy dimple comes out to play. "Yeah, like you're the star of a parade. Haven't you ever ridden in a Homecoming parade?"

I giggle. "Something tells me that you and I had very different high school experiences, Jake."

I take my shoes off and climb onto the back of his car, the metal warm under my skirt. As soon as I'm settled, Jake kicks his boots off until he's in black socks and climbs beside me.

"This would be romantic under other circumstances," I say, looking at the sky as he grabs one of my hands.

The moon is bright, but some stars are still visible. Wind ruffles my hair, and I close my eyes at the beauty of a perfect Halloween night. I breathe in the cool night air, crisp but not uncomfortable enough to need a coat.

He turns my hand over and opens a pack of antibiotic ointment, squeezing the clear substance out and using the paper container to smear it around the injured area. "Is it weird that I still think this is romantic?"

"Do all of your dates run away from you and make an ass of themselves?" I ask.

"Ironically, yes. This is par for the course."

"Somehow, I think you're lying." There's no way this gorgeous man frightens women off. "Tell me the worst date you've had."

"Other than any I had with Millie?"

"Sure," I chuckle.

He shrugs and smiles a wry grin that only lifts half his mouth. "I'm not always the most confident person. Hence, you had to talk to me first. I think a lot of women want that confident swagger in a man, you know? I'm awkward on dates, always worried about impressing a woman and if I'm doing the right things. I spend so much time in my own head, worrying about doing the right things, that I do the wrong things. I get a lot of first dates, but I don't get many second dates."

"Something tells me that's their loss."

He clears his throat and opens an adhesive bandage package. "Want to tell me what happened back there?"

I eye his witch hunter costume and shake my head. "Tell me why you're dressed like a witch hunter first."

He tilts his head and bites his lip. "Witch hunter? Is that what I look like?"

"Isn't that what your costume is?"

He laughs, and I like the sound of it. It's boyish and light like he doesn't have a care in the world. That must be nice. "Here I thought I looked like a Pilgrim."

"Pilgrims didn't wear ammunition casing across their chest," I say, gesturing across my own torso and nodding at his bandolier. "My mother used to read stories to me about witch hunters. You look like one of them."

He takes his hat and bandolier off and tosses both into the front seat, running his hands through his hair to straighten it. "See this stain here?" he asks, pointing to his chest. "I wore this suit to a funeral a couple of years ago, and Millie threw hot sauce on me. I only wore the bandolier to cover the stain."

I chuckle as he grabs my other hand, and I twist toward him so he can put the antibiotic cream on my hand. "She's a piece of work, huh?"

"That she is," he mutters, concentrating on taking care of my hand.

It's nice that he's doing this. I've always taken care of myself. At least, I've taken care of myself since my mom died. Even when she was alive, nobody has cleaned a scrape or put a Band-Aid on me since I was little.

"You're really kind for putting up with all of this for me on our so-called first date," I say.

"Putting up with what exactly?"

I let him bandage my other hand, and he moves to my leg. "Is this OK?" he asks, lifting up my skirt past my knee. I nod and adjust the tulle skirt, lifting the cocktail dress under it. His hand is warm on my knee, and I slide my skirt up further, signaling that I'd let him touch higher if he wants. His warm fingers make my heart pound, and I put a bandaged hand over my chest like I can calm it from the outside.

"I made Millie stop talking," I whisper.

He lifts his head to stare at me. "What are you talking about? How?"

I shrug. "You know the coy pond story?"

"Sure. Everyone in town does."

"It's true. I boiled the coy."

He laughs a little and focuses back on my knee. "Sure, Eliza."

"I'm serious. I don't know what happened."

"I do," he says. "Something in the man-made pond's system short-circuited. The filter or temperature monitoring system malfunctioned. You didn't mass murder fish, Eliza."

"Weird things happen on Halloween, Jake."

"Like what?"

"Like me wishing your ex-girlfriend would shut the fuck up, and she suddenly shuts the fuck up."

He turns and looks back at the convention center like he just realized there's still a party going on in there and he left his tongueless ex-girlfriend in there with his sexist roommate. He blinks and stares at the door a few moments before turning back to me. "Not possible," he says, shaking his head. "Magic isn't real."

"I assure you that it's very real. I watched my mother use it every day until the day she died."

"How do you know she wasn't tricking you?"

"Like my entire life was one big magic show?"

He nods. "Something like that. Slide of hand. Look at one hand while she does something with another."

"It didn't work like that," I chuckle. "She fixed relationships. She made sterile people fertile better than fertility drugs."

His forehead scrunches. "Maybe those people in the bad relationship fixed their problems because they decided to communicate with each other. People with fertility issues conceive all the time. There's a reason some babies are surprises."

"You're really that much of a skeptic?"

"If I see something really fantastic happen, I'll admit that I'm wrong," he says, placing a bandage on my knee and wiping his finger across it a little more than necessary to get it to stick. His hand caresses the top of my knee before pulling my tutu down. "All better."

If he asked to kiss it and make it feel better, I'd let him. A chill moves up my spine, and I've never felt so taken care of by a man. Most men aren't chivalrous, kind, and this gorgeous. My fingers clench with the itch to grab his hot sauce-covered lapel and stick my tongue down his throat.

"You didn't hurt Millie," he says, bringing me out of my thoughts of kissing those perfect and masculine lips.

"I made her tongue disappear."

He laughs. "She probably swallowed it."

"That doesn't actually happen, Jake."

"Neither does a witch waving a wand and making someone's tongue disappear."

"I don't have a wand," I deadpan. "I've never needed one. Mom didn't, either. She used spells and potions. Intention is the most important, and I intended for your ex to shut up."

He smirks at me and pushes a tendril of my hair back from my face. "Alright, I believe that you believe you're magic, and that makes things happen. It's like people having a positive attitude and things change for them."

He moves closer to me and shrugs out of his jacket, wrapping it around my shoulders and straightening it over my torso. "I should have done that earlier. Sorry if you were cold."

"I wasn't cold."

"You were shivering," he murmurs.

"I'm shivering because a sexy man just bandaged my hands and knees like a knight in witch hunting armor."

He chuckles and smiles. "Did you call me sexy?"

"You have to know that you're hot."

"People say that," he says, shaking his head. "I've just never really believed it. I always see someone else as better looking, smarter, or a better boyfriend."

"I think you're handsome and kind. Not every man would risk blood contamination for a woman that can't even run away without tripping and falling."

He reaches out and runs his finger up my jaw from my chin to my ear. "Can I tell you a secret?" he asks as I lean into his warm finger. "I told you that I saw you at your candle shop when I subbed for your carrier. That was true. What I didn't tell you is that I walked into your store and thought you were the most beautiful woman I've ever seen in my life. When you came over to my table tonight, I was shocked you walked over to talk to me. That's why I spilled my drink. It wasn't your fault, but it startled me."

My hands act on their own, and I put my hands on his chest, his heart pounding under my fingers. He tilts my chin up and dips his lips toward me as my eyes flutter closed. His breath is on my lips and smells of the whiskey he drank and something minty like a breath mint. His lips brush mine softly, and I wrap my arms around him, ready to drink him in fully.

"Ughghhhghghg," someone moans behind us,

and a clutch purse hits Jake in the cheek and bounces into my lap. Millie runs over to the car, climbs over the trunk, and grabs the back of Jake's jacket. Her skin squeaks against metal as she climbs over the car's exterior. "Moer Ucr!" she yells, shaking him.

"Shit, Millie. Let go!" Jake yells just as Paul catches up to Millie and pulls her off Jake's suit. "I'm sorry about your tongue, but it's not my fault."

Millie nods and sticks both of her middle fingers up. "Es I is, aole!"

"What is she saying?" Jake asks, looking from Paul to me.

"I think she said, 'Yes it is, asshole.' Just my guess. I also think she called you a mother fucker when she hit you with the purse," I say.

"Hmm. That's interesting you understood that," Jake says.

"I'm working mostly off vowels and body language with those guesses."

"Millie, this isn't helpful," Jake says, facing her. "If you want a ride to the hospital so they can find your tongue, I'll drive you. Get in. I'll drop you off."

"I'll just go. This night has been really weird," I say, climbing to the front seat of Jake's convertible.

"Please don't go, Eliza. I can drive Millie to the hospital. Then, I want to get to know you better."

"Agugugugugh," Millie grunts, grabbing Jake's lapel.

Jake looks at me like he wants me to translate, and I shrug. "I have no idea on that one."

Paul pulls her hands off Jake's lapel again and nudges her into the backseat of Jake's car. I stare at Millie, red-faced and still crying, and feel sorry for her. Paul walks back to his job inside the conference center without a word, and I watch until he gets through the doors. Is he really just going to leave Millie with us?

Millie crosses her arms and grits her teeth as she stares at Jake, but there's something in her eyes. Maybe it's unrequited love, or maybe it's the absolute terror of not having a tongue any longer. I did this to her, and I need to fix it.

"Jake, take me to my house. Let me try to fix Millie. The hospital won't be able to help her."

Millie hears me and groans as she lifts up her naughty nurse skirt to wipe her nose, flashing Jake and me. We avert our eyes, and Jake bites his lip before sitting in the driver's seat. "I really think the hospital can find her tongue."

"If I can't fix her, we can go to the hospital."

"What if she digests her tongue or something in the meantime?"

"Or Uhs ake," Millie grunts, and Jake scratches his head.

"She said, 'For fuck's sake.' I guess she doesn't believe I can fix her either."

"This is ridiculous," he says, pushing his key into the ignition and starting the car. "She needs a hospital. You can't fix a lost tongue with salt, pepper, and cinnamon sticks."

I place my hand on his forearm, squeezing a little. He turns to me with dark eyes, and I know he wants my touch as much as I want his. Damn, I wanted to kiss him. It's just going to have to wait.

"Go to my house. Let me try to fix Millie, and let me show you that magic is real."

CHAPTER 6

Jake

"What are we looking for?" I ask, tossing aside boxes and setting them in rows. Packing tape crisscrosses the top of them, and Eliza pulls more boxes and plastic storage containers off a creaky metal shelf.

"A big black book. It's my mother's grimoire."

"What's that?"

"It's a witch's spell book. A witch's grimoire is sacred to them, with a lot of their own spells and potions added to it over time. My mother experimented in the kitchen and would write everything down. It may have a spell or potion for Millie," she explains, wiping her hands on her cheeks.

The dirt on her fingers leaves light smudges that I want to wipe off, but I don't touch her. Partly because Millie sits on the basement stairs a few feet away, red-faced and cracking her knuckles.

"Millie, you could help. Eliza's doing all this for you," I say as we stare at each other.

Her lip curls in response. "Ugh oo."

"Was that 'fuck you?'" I ask, hands on hips.

"Yep," Eliza mumbles behind me. "I know it's here somewhere."

"I'm getting better at understanding cuss words she grunts," I say, turning back to Eliza. "What are you going to do when we find this grimoire thing?"

"Look at it, of course."

"If it was so important to your mom, why is it in a dusty old box in the basement?"

Eliza's face crinkles, and she sits on a large box. Dust puffs into the air, and she waves her hand in front of her face before wiping a tear from her eye.

"Shit, Eliza," I say, moving boxes aside so I can sit next to her. "I didn't mean it that way. I'm sorry."

She wipes another tear and puts her head in her hands as I rub her back in circles and try not to think about how good her warm back feels through her dress. "It's OK," she mumbles. "You just said what I was already thinking. I hid it away after her funeral. I couldn't bear to look at it. Some people hide pictures after a person dies because they can't look at them every day. I couldn't walk by that book without seeing her over it and writing in it. It hurt, you know?"

I nod, but I don't really understand. Sure, my grandmother died, and I was sad. Grandparents die, though. It wasn't a surprise, and I found her pictures and things more comforting than hurtful. It must be different when it is someone that isn't old or expected to die.

"It also reminded me that I'm a complete failure."

I wrinkle my eyes and stop stroking her back. "That can't be true."

"Look what I did to poor Millie," she says, gesturing to my ex-girlfriend as Millie holds up her middle finger.

Millie's been doing that a lot in the last hour since the tongue swallowing incident happened. When we were dating, she only flipped people off in traffic. I wonder if she's getting tired of grunting to communicate and is just using hand signals.

"I'm still not convinced you did this."

She raises her head. "Do you really think my mother gaslighted me my whole life and blamed everything on magical powers? Because I saw stuff, Jake. I saw things that couldn't be explained by science. My mother lit candles with her fingers. I know," she holds up her hands when I open my mouth. "You think she had a secret third hand holding a lighter that I didn't see. You'll tell me there's a scientific explanation for it. I know what I saw. I know the power I grew up watching. I've even felt it inside of myself before something inevitably went wrong. It's real. I'm going to prove it to you."

She stands up and rustles her dress, and I sigh when I stand up next to her. I can't believe I just insulted the woman I've lusted after for a full year. "Show me, then. I want to believe you. I want to see something magical. Hell, don't worry about good magic. Show me the shitty kind. Just let me see something so I can believe you and help you."

She focuses on the concrete wall across the room, her hands flexing like they're asleep. "Eliza?" I whisper.

She ignores me and plucks a hair from her head, grimacing with the removal, and opens her phone. She scrolls through her pictures until she finds a photo of a middle-aged woman with gray hair and blue eyes. The eyes are different, but this must be Eliza's mother because she looks just like Eliza will probably look in twenty-five years.

Eliza holds her hair out to nothing, pointing it like they did in old movies when they tried to find water with sticks. It sags and hangs loosely from her fingers. "Book that's bound to the one I see, wake and show yourself to me," Eliza mutters, moving her plucked hair slowly back and forth across the basement.

Millie grunts from her spot on the stairs, and she's wide-eyed with fear. I shake my head at her and shrug back at her.

"Uh, is that a real spell? It sounds like something from *Charmed*."

"It doesn't have to be a real spell. Sure, those are effective, but it's intention that matters. My mom's picture tells the universe I need something associated with her. My hair is mine. It's like the spells my mom wrote in her grimoire. They were *her* spells because of intention. Not something she found in a tourist trap shop that sells witch supplies."

When moments pass and nothing happens, Eliza flutters her eyes and rolls her neck. "I know you hear me," she murmurs.

She squares her shoulders and bites her lips. "Show me, now!" she yells, causing Millie and me to jump with the loud echo in the closed basement.

"It's fine, Eliza. I still like you and want to get to know..."

"Stop, Jake," she mutters. "Look."

She nods at the hair in her hand that's pointing straight out in the direction of the tool bench. Eliza walks around boxes, following the direction the hair leads her.

"That's just static. You're wearing tulle, and it's dry down here for a basement. How do you do that, by the way?" I ask. "My basement leaks like a paper boat."

"No, Jake. Look!" she says as we approach a tall tool chest with built-in bench. The hair changes direction, pointing up. "Not static electricity."

"It still could be," I grumble. I'm not ready to admit that magic exists. It can't. Such knowledge would turn the world upside down.

"If that book is behind the top cabinet door, will you believe me?"

I look at her bare arms. She doesn't have sleeves to hide anything up there. "If a hair told you where this grimoire thing is, I'll concede that it may be... weird."

Eliza sighs and drops the hair to the floor. She walks to the tool bench and climbs on it like she's reaching for a jar on a kitchen shelf. The door sticks, but when she finally gets it open, there's a large black book on the highest shelf.

"Can you reach it for me?" she asks, reaching up so that her skirt rises a couple of inches. I catch a glimpse of tiny black panties, and I have the sudden urge to take them off with my teeth.

I'm a little over six feet tall, but I still have to pull myself onto the bench to reach the top shelf. I bring the book down to Eliza, and she blows the thin layer of dust off it. "It looks like something from five hundred years ago," I say.

She looks at me and immediately flicks her eyes away. "I may have failed to mention that this book is about four hundred years old."

"Christ! You put a four-hundred-year-old book in a tool chest in a Midwestern basement? At least put it in a plastic baggie or something."

"Looking back, it probably wasn't the best idea. My mother would be horrified," she says, walking the book over to a nearby plastic tub full of Christmas decorations and sitting on it. She holds the book in her lap and gently opens the cover. It cracks like the leather binding is so old that it may break in half.

I pull up another storage bin and sit next to her. "Can I see what a four-century-old magical book looks like, or is this for family only?"

She shrugs. "Mom never told me to keep it a secret. My dad knew about all of this."

I clear my throat. "Where is your dad?"

Her eyes glaze over for a minute, but I can't look away from her. Millie also listens, her squinted eyes focused on Eliza.

"My father never could wrap his head around the whole witch thing. They were in love once. I was born out of that love. But when Mom told him I have power, he kind of freaked out," she sighs, shaking her head like there are cobwebs in it. "He left a few weeks later."

"I'm sorry, Eliza," I say, putting my hand on top of hers only to hear a disapproving grunt from Millie. I pull my hand away and nail Millie with a dirty look. "Do you have contact with him?"

"He sends me birthday cards, and he paid child

support until I was eighteen. He paid for one year of community college. He never shirked making sure I had food or clothing, but he never made an effort to see me. He married another woman when I was about ten. I've never met her."

"For what it's worth, he may have fed and clothed you, but I think he's a huge asshole. Personally, I don't see how anyone, let alone your own father, would not want to spend time with you."

She looks up at me, and there's a tear in the corner of her eye. She grins and runs her hand over the book on her lap. "Thanks, Jake. That means a lot."

She pages through the book, and I try to stay silent, letting her think or search for what she needs. I glance at Millie, and her arms are wrapped around her knees as she watches Eliza with hopeful eyes.

Eliza's book is written in old-fashioned handwriting and full of symbols I don't understand. Large loops and tiny squiggles cause her to squint, getting close to the book to read the faded letters. She flips through pages and follows arrows with her fingertip.

It seems like minutes have turned to hours when she perks up, sitting up straight on the storage box. "I think this may be it."

"You found something?" I ask.

Millie's eyes widen and she lifts her head.

"It's a potion," she says, dragging her fingers down the page and repeating odd ingredients under her breath.

"Is it hard to make? Do I have to decapitate a chicken to get parts? If so, can we use a rotisserie chicken from the grocery store in a pinch?"

She reads a few more seconds before closing the book and holding it to her chest. She walks to the stairs. "No chickens have to die for this potion. I should have everything up in my mother's pantry. I haven't been in there much since she died, but it was well-stocked."

Millie moves out of the way so Eliza can pass her up the stairs, and I marvel that Millie didn't try to trip her. She must be desperate to get her tongue back. Millie stands and follows Eliza up the stairs, and I turn off the overhead light and follow the ladies, determined to help in any way that I can. I'm unsure of what I saw with the hair, but I'm going to go into the kitchen with an open mind about witch potions.

CHAPTER 7

Eliza

"I need some eye of newt," I mumble loud enough for Jake to hear, a slight grin across my face.

He clears his throat. "Do you really have newt eyes in your pantry?"

"I'm just fucking with you, Jake. Eye of newt is actually a mustard seed. I'm sure some witch along the line thought it just sounded scary and wanted to fuck with their raffle date, too. For example, when someone mentions an adder's fork, it isn't a snake tongue. It's just violet."

Jake puts his hand over his chest and blows out a breath. Millie walks over to my kitchen counter and slides onto one of the bar stools. She looks around my kitchen with wide eyes and taps her fingers on my granite countertop.

"Don't worry, Millie. I think this will fix you. Just hang tight so I can take time and get it right."

I hope everything I said is true, but I don't have a lot of faith in myself. I'm amazing at candles in my shop. I can bless them, say spells over them, and make good things happen for the people that burn them. I've just never been great with potions. Mixing potions was my mom's thing, and she was able to whip up anything with very little mess, bottling the liquid neatly in a glass bottle. She measured things diligently, recording results of the most minute ingredient changes.

My strength is more along the lines of blessing hot wax and hoping for the best before I sell it as a Kwanzaa candle.

Jake walks around my kitchen, opening pantry doors and touching jars and containers. He picks up several, frowns, and places them back on my shelves as I rummage through my pots and pans. I set a pan on the counter and turn the burner on low under it.

"What does this stuff do?" Jake asks, holding up a jar.

"It's peanut butter."

He holds it back from his face. "Why does it look weird and not have a label?"

"It's from the health food store where you grind your own nuts into butter. Then, you stir it each time you use it. That's why it looks funny."

He places the jar back on the shelf and picks up another container of crushed greenery. "Is this like moss with bat shit on it or something?" he asks, smiling.

I stifle a giggle. "No, Jake. That's my weed stash."

"Your house is exceptionally interesting."

"Are you going to let me work or ask what every jar on my shelf is?" I ask with a smile.

Jake closes my pantry door and claps his hands together. "I will let you work. Can I help?"

"Actually, you can. I need to constantly stir this stuff and may need you to hand me things."

Jake pulls himself up on the counter, and I don't even grimace at the thought of someone's butt on my countertop like I usually would. "You know, this is our date night. I technically won you. We should take time to get to know each other," he says, grinning.

"Because we haven't got to know each other with me making your ex-girlfriend's tongue disappear, you bandaging me in your car, or searching my basement for a four-hundred-year-old book? I also won you, by the way. When you say you won me, that sounds like you played poker for a night with a man's prostitute."

"Ok, not your typical first date. I'll admit that. But who wants typical? This night has already been one adventure after another. Personally, I'm excited to see what happens next."

"Let's hope it's me fixing Millie."

Millie grunts in response and puts her head down on the counter with a whimper. I don't like the woman, but I want to pat her back and tell her it will be OK. I just hope it's true.

Jake stirs the soup pot as I add the ingredients of pressed oils, crushed seeds and flowers, and lavender. "What exactly are you making? A returning potion?"

"Something like that. I'm going to make a simple voice tincture known for giving voice to people that have lost theirs for whatever reason. It should also protect her from any curses and revert any that she could already be under. Hand me the apples from the fruit basket behind you," I say, nodding at the bananas, oranges, and apples that are usually my breakfast.

"How does an apple give Millie her tongue back?" he asks, handing me a bright red apple.

His hand touches mine as he hands me the fruit, and a shiver moves up my back. He doesn't pull away right away but drags his fingers across my hand like a feather. The movement across my skin, the warmth of his own body, and the pressure he uses; this is a man that knows how to touch a woman. It's been so long since I've had a man in my bed, or kitchen even, that knows how to touch a woman and isn't selfish. His eyes are dark and full of want, and I momentarily wish I'd just made Millie disappear entirely.

Millie grunts again, jolting me out of my sex thoughts about Jake. A flush moves up my neck, and I clear my throat. "Apples are protective."

Millie and Jake both tilt their head to the side. "Apples?" Jake asks.

"Sure," I say, cutting into the apple as my mother taught me to do as a girl, with the seeds perfectly divided on each side of the cut and careful not to slice a seed. "The witches of old used to make amulets out of apple tree wood and give them to children. It was supposed to give the children long life."

"Did it work?"

"Maybe for the children. The witches were drowned, burned, or found themselves hanging from a tree. People didn't like amulets given to children from what were called wise women by some."

"That's fascinating," Jake says, stirring the oils as I add apple seeds and peel the skin. "So, some women thought witches were wise?"

"The word witch comes from 'wise woman' and a lot of other people thought these women were wise. They went to the village wise woman for a lot of things like fertility issues, controlling pregnancy, ending pregnancies with herbs, and even poisoning abusive husbands and fathers," I explain, tears forming in my eyes just thinking about how my ancestors were treated.

"Midwives were even called witches when they

saved the lives of the women in dangerous childbirth. People couldn't explain how these women did it, so it must be evil magic against God's will. You can imagine that the men of the time didn't like a woman being able to control pregnancy or even being able to control a childbirth outcome. In reality, the woman was just really good at herbs and knowing what a plant could do, poisonous plants for abusive husbands included."

"It was fear that caused hatred for these women?" Jake asks, stirring the potion in the pan as it changes from red to a brown color.

"At the end of the day, fear causes all hatred."

Jake frowns and looks off in the distance like I've just said something really wise.

"The Salem witch trials came at a time when things were changing, getting more progressive for the time. It scared some people that wanted to keep things the same. They couldn't explain some new things, and people were starting to doubt the church. The men in power couldn't have that. Also, people were starting to question government decisions that were accepted before. Ironically, it was also a period of unusually cold weather that had to be blamed on something since the science of the time couldn't explain it. Women were scapegoats."

"You know a lot about this."

"Some of my ancestors, the very people that wrote in that book, ended up on the wrong side of a rope for it," I mutter. "I'm a little sensitive about my family's knowledge that's been passed down."

He reaches for me, stroking my arm and leaving his hand on my shoulder. Not even Millie grunts in objection to the comforting gesture.

Steam rises from the pot, and I turn the burner off with a click. I pull open a nearby drawer and find one of the vials my mother used for potions and ladle the brown, mucky-looking substance into the bottle, the hot liquid burning my hand through the glass.

"Does she try it now?" Jake asks.

"Yes, but we need to do it under the full light of the moon and in a wide-open place of nature. We can go to the dog park next door."

Jake slides off the counter, and Millie gets up from her stool so quickly that the stool falls to the ground. She rights it and walks to the door ahead of us, pulling the door open and looking back to check if we're coming. Jake and I walk behind her, and he slips his hand into mine, his fingers sliding between my own as we follow Millie out onto the porch.

Millie doesn't notice that Jake holds my hand as we walk to the small dog park next to my house. She undoes the gate on the chain-length fence and marches to the center of the grassy area, looking up at the moon and letting out a whine like she's praying. I follow mutely, not able to speak because of the warmth of Jake's hand.

When we meet up with Millie, Jake brings my hand to his mouth and kisses it. "Knock em' dead, Eliza."

"Uh, please don't say that. I made her tongue disappear, but I really don't want to kill her."

He laughs. "You know what I meant."

I step to Millie and look up at the moon. It's full and right over us, and I flex my fingers. Something about the moon, in general, makes me feel powerful. Always has. To have it full on Halloween, my most powerful night of the year, makes electric zaps move up and down my spine when I stand under it.

"I need a hair from you, Millie. I need something of yours to put in the potion."

She pulls a single hair from her head, much like I did to my own earlier, and holds it over the vial in my outstretched hand. She looks at me one last time, shrugs, and drops the hair into the potion right as a strong wind picks up.

"Oo I ink i?" Millie grunts.

"Yes," I say, nodding. "You drink it in one go. Like a shot. It's not going to taste good. But seeing as you don't have a tongue with taste buds, you'll just have to worry about the aftertaste." Millie shrugs.

"I'm going to bless it first, and you both need to be quiet. Your words can combine with mine and do who knows what."

Jake and Millie both nod, and I bow my head and clasp the vial in both hands. I mumble the blessing words under my breath and put intention into the vial that this will work for the good of Millie, not myself.

Heat blooms in my chest, and I feel the power I've known all my life, chaotic as it is at times. It's still the power of my ancestors. The power pulses through my body but ends at my fingertips, and something I can't identify doesn't quite fully transfer. Frustration blooms in my chest, and I hope my intention and the potion will be enough for Millie.

As soon as the words are done, I hold out the vial. "Face the moon when you drink it."

"Why does she have to face the moon?" Jake asks behind me.

"It shows respect for the moon," I deadpan.

"Of course. Silly me," he says, his brow creased and a slight grin on his lips. He still doesn't believe.

Millie throws her head back and drinks the tonic in one gulp. As soon as she swallows, I close my eyes, hoping with every fiber of my being that this works. Wind rustles my hair a little, and silence stretches for seconds that feel like hours.

"Did it work, Millie?" Jake whispers behind me.

More silence follows, but I still can't stand to look at her. I don't know how I'll face her if it didn't work. Hell, I don't know how I'll face this amazing guy I met tonight. Talk about embarrassing.

"I think it did," a voice that isn't Jake's says, and my eyes pop open. Millie rubs her hand over her mouth and sticks her tongue out like Gene Simmons, wiggling it. "Is it ere?" she asks.

Jake hugs me, picking me up and swinging me around. "It worked. Holy shit. You made her tongue appear. How?"

"Do you believe me now?" I ask as he sets me down on the ground. Jake's speechless, and Millie works her jaw from side to side. Jake's eyes flitter around the area like he's seeing the world with new eyes, and he runs his hands through his hair.

"I don't know what to believe. You'll have to give me a second to process this, Eliza. It's like being told unicorns are real."

"Uh..."

"Don't tell me that. I'm not ready for it," he says, holding up a hand.

I do a happy dance and clap my hands at Millie, but I'm really clapping for me. My magic worked properly. For the first time in forever, my magic worked like it was supposed to. My mom would be so proud of me, and I send up a silent prayer to wherever she is. I, Eliza Owl, performed correct magic on Halloween when I usually fuck up everything. Maybe I just needed to mature a little.

"Uh, Eliza?" Jake asks, his head cocked to the side and looking around the neighborhood, turning in his spot. Millie does the same, still palming her lips to make sure everything in her mouth is there. "Do you hear that?"

I stop clapping and turn around, straining my ears to hear what he's talking about. I only hear barking dogs. Lots of barking dogs. In fact, it sounds like a barking and snarling wolf pack as it gets louder around the neighborhood, moving in waves as the barking spreads.

"What is that?" I ask, not really expecting them to have an answer.

Millie looks at the empty vial in her hand. "Uh, Eliza? Is there any possibility that I also drank dog hair in this vial?"

I turn in a circle, looking at the ground around me. We're in a dog park, and it's possible that a dog hair came into contact with the potion the same way hers did, especially when the wind picked up. "Fuck!" I yell, covering my face with my hands.

Embarrassment replaces my joy almost immediately as the dog sound intensifies. Every dog in town barks, growls, or howls. The sound gets so loud that Jake covers his ears and nearby neighbors step out onto their porches, looking up and down the street. Tears fill my eyes, and heat burns my face. I thought I had it, but I can't do a fucking thing right.

I look at Jake with apologetic eyes, a tear leaking down my face. He steps toward me and reaches out, but I back away. "Don't come near me. I could hurt you."

"Eliza, you fixed Millie. You can fix this. Let's go look at this book your mom had," he suggests, nodding back at my house. "It'll have something about controlling dogs, right?"

I shake my head, and suddenly want to sleep on the ground as exhaustion fills my body. The idea of going back in to do more research is like the time I got a D in a college philosophy course and was told I had to take the entire thing over again the next semester.

I pull away from Jake when he walks toward me, holding his arms out like he's going to hug me. "Eliza, I just want to help. We can do this."

"No, Jake, stay away," I beg and do the only thing I can think of. I turn and run for the common ground woods behind the dog park.

The ground crunches under my feet until I get near the trees, and I vault over a mossy log with Jake hot on my heels. "Eliza, let's talk about this. It can be fixed, right?" he asks, his voice choppy with his labored breathing from running after me.

My shoes sink into the mud as I keep running. I know these woods like the back of my hand, but Jake is faster. He grabs my shoulder and spins me around until we both fall into a tree, catching ourselves on the bark and fumbling through the darkness until I feel his arm. I pull back like his arm burned me, and I straighten up to run toward the old barn I know is about a quarter mile from here. I can hide there.

"Stop, Eliza. Why won't you talk to me?"

"I fuck up everything I touch. No wonder everyone hates me. Don't you wonder why Lily Jane's my only friend?"

"I don't hate you. Do I not count as a person?" he asks, his voice tender. His words make my heart skip a beat.

"Of course, you count. You seem like a great guy. But you can't possibly know what you're getting into with me, Jake. Go!" I say, pushing his chest.

He doesn't move and doesn't turn to leave. I squint to see his profile in the darkness. With his dark suit and dark hair, I only see his white dress suit at times as the moon dances in and out of the clouds.

I push him again and feel horrid. "Please, just go. You need to go back and get Millie home."

"I don't care about Millie!" he yells. "I mean, sure, I cared that her tongue was gone and wanted that fixed, but you did it. Let's go back and fix the dogs."

"I can't!" I scream and run my hands through my hair in anguish. "I fuck up everything I touch. I don't want to hurt you. Why can't you see that?"

He grabs my shoulders, "Eliza, stop fighting with me and come help us."

The moon moves behind a cloud, and I take my opportunity to slip from his grasp and silently move to the side. Turning, I step out of his reach and move behind a nearby tree. "Eliza? Where did you go?" he asks, a rustling sound coming from his pants. He must be looking for his phone. "Please don't do this."

"Go, Jake," I say, taking a few more steps and hiding behind another tree. Jake's feet shuffle nearby, and I'm reminded of the *Marco Polo* game Lily Jane and I used to play at the community pool as children. I bite my lip so I won't make any noise to signal where I am.

My heart pounds in my temple, and tears burn my cheek. No other guy has ever come after me except that time two kids in seventh grade chased me down only to throw their cherry slushes into my back. It's all I can do to not run back to him and let him hold me. His hugs are probably the kind women dream about with strong arms and promises of safety.

I can't promise he's safe with me, though.

I push off the tree trunk and pray for soft earth under my feet as I run away from him further. Luck smiles on me as wet leaves sink under my shoes and no dry leaves or sticks give away my location.

He calls for me for several minutes, moving parallel to my run, and I almost call for him. The light from his phone's flashlight app swings left and right, but never in my direction. I move from tree to tree when he points his light away from my location.

Eventually, I move far enough away from him that I know he won't see me through the thick woods. Distant howling and barking are the only sounds in the woods as I run through the trees and don't stop until I get to a deserted soybean field.

CHAPTER 8

Jake

"Where did she go?" Millie asks when I walk back to the dog park.

I shake my head. "I don't know. I lost her in the woods. I can't see a damn thing." I run my hands through my hair, removing sticks and leaves from running through thickets. This can't be happening again. Why does she always run from me? "It's a full moon, but it's dark as fuck under the tree cover. Maybe she'll come back in a few minutes."

Millie and I wait, and she taps her feet impatiently, holding her hands to her ears when the dog howling gets close. Looking around at Eliza's neighboring houses, the neighbors stand on their porches with phones up to one ear and fingers stuck in their other. Who do they think will fix this? The police? They can't do anything but start tranquilizing dogs or something, and that probably wouldn't work anyway. Are the neighbors calling the fire department? I guess that would be the best bet since they get cats out of trees. I'm not sure how they would get dogs to stop barking and howling, though.

"Do we have to wait for her, or can we just go to your house and have hot sex to celebrate getting back together?" Millie asks, and I rear back like she punched me.

"I'm not having sex with you, Millie. We're not getting back together."

"Why not?" she whines, and I second guess the decision to give her tongue back. She rubs her hands up my shirt and tries to kiss my chin.

I push her away and grab her shoulders, holding her arm's length from me. "We broke up two years ago, Millie. We're not getting back together, and we're not fucking."

"I'm not waiting all night for the woman you have a boner for when you can have all this," she says, waving her hand up and down her body and cocking her hip. Her face is red, and she crinkles her nose like she does when she's mad.

I ignore her and turn in a circle, thinking. "I'm going to drive you back to the charity event. Your car's there anyway. Maybe she'd go back there and talk to Lily Jane," I say, walking to my car. Millie's shoes clack behind me once we reach the sidewalk, but I make sure to walk ahead of her. I don't need her grabbing my hand and Eliza choosing that moment to come back and find us. "Even if she's not there, maybe Lily Jane would have an idea where she went."

Millie and I get into my convertible, and I nod

toward the backseat. "Get in the back like you did when you rode here."

"I will not. That's ridiculous."

"You're just going to try to jerk me off or give me road head the entire way there. Get in back. I don't need a car accident tonight."

"You used to like those things," she mumbles, her hands moving her naughty nurse skirt up her thighs. I put my hand over hers to stop her from showing me her goodies, and she tries to hold my hand. I shake her off like I have fly paper stuck to my fingers.

"I still like those things. Just not from you. I don't consent to have you touch me, and I don't want to deal with fighting you off."

Something breaks, and her face crumbles. "You really don't want me, do you?" she asks, cupping her face in her hands.

"Millie," I sigh. I can't believe I'm dealing with this while Eliza is out in the woods somewhere. "There's a reason we broke up. We're not meant to be together. It's been two years. You need to move on. Hell, you need to let me move on. I'm going to drop you off, and then I'm going to find Eliza and ask her out on a real date after the shit show night of this one. You need to suck it up, and go out with your raffle date. If it doesn't work out with Paul, and I apologize in advance for everything he will say to you tonight, you'll need to find someone else that's a better fit for you. But we are over, and you need to respect that. Capiche?"

She ignores me but climbs into the backseat with a hiccup. I start the car and rev the engine as I back out of Eliza's driveway. Millie sobs the short drive to the conference center and jumps out as soon as we reach the parking lot. I'd normally tell her goodbye and to enjoy her night as she climbs out of the car, but I can't wait to see the back of her.

As soon as I kill the engine, I unbuckle my seatbelt and sprint to the convention center doors. Once inside, it's like I never left. The past hour has felt like a decade to me, and I blink my eyes, processing that people are still in the same clothes and some are even in the same spot they were in when I left.

The raffle table is gone, but raffle dates still mill about the area, grinning and having polite conversation about jobs, pets, and where they went to high school or college. I shove my way through the crowd and instantly sweat with the proximity of hot bodies in the closed space.

Paul is at his station at the appetizer table, droopy-eyed and stirring a pot of marinara sauce for the mozzarella sticks. He holds up the spoon and lets the red sauce drip into the pan as he stares at it, watching drops plop into the container with a smile. I don't think he'll be much help in his current state, but I don't see Lily Jane.

"Paul!" I yell as I get closer to the table.

He looks up and around, squinting at the chandelier above him. "Ha. Someone's talking to me. Is that you, universe?"

"Yes, Paul. This is God," I say in my best James Earl Jones impression, standing right next to him. "Jake will appear in front of you, and you need to tell him where Lily Jane is."

"Whoa," he moans, looking at the ceiling and following the disco ball shimmers with his eyes. "OK, God."

When he looks away and notices me, his eyes widen. "Dude! God just told me I'd see you."

"Is that so? Do you happen to know where Lily Jane is?"

He nods and grabs a mozzarella stick out of the catering pan with his bare hand. He sticks it in his mouth and chews, trying to remember where she is. Hell, he may be trying to remember *who* she is. He squints and swallows the mozzarella stick and reaches for a new one. "Yeah, man. I saw her off to the side of the stage a little bit ago. I think she's a band groupie or something. Have you seen my date?"

"I just dropped her off. She's here. I told her to have a great time with you tonight."

"Did you get her tongue back?" he asks, and I'm surprised he remembers that.

"Yeah, she has her tongue."

"Nice! I can't go out with a girl without a tongue," he says, shaking his head. "I'm going to see if I can find her."

He walks off, forgetting his catering job in the process, and I eye the empty pans of appetizers nearby. Either the crowd is extra hungry, or Paul hasn't been refilling the supply. Great. I don't need him fired. Adding an unemployed roommate to my list of worries would make this night worse, and I'm not sure this night *can* get any worse.

I push my way through the crowd of people dancing and the long line for the bar. The band is covering an old Poison song, and beer sloshes on me as I walk past the dance floor. People in their forties rock out to the songs, singing along and pushing against each other to the rhythm of the music. I can't focus on anyone, and faces blur in front of me as I keep moving through the crowd on a mission.

I emerge from the dance floor and find Lily Jane at the side of the stage, swaying her hips and mouthing along with the lyrics. I tap her on the shoulder, and she turns around with a frown, her forehead furrowed. "Can I help you?"

"Have you seen Eliza?"

"And...who are you?"

Heat moves up my neck. Of course. I know who

she is, but she doesn't know me. "I'm sorry," I say, holding out my hand for her to shake. "My name is Jake Salt, and I'm Eliza's raffle date for the night."

She shakes my hand with a firm, professional grip. "Nice to meet you. Are you having a good time?"

"Well," I mutter, running my hand up the back of my head. My hair is sweaty, and I wipe my hand on my pants. "I kind of lost her."

"What do you mean you lost her?" she gasps. Her eyes go wide, and she brings a hand to her chest.

"Some stuff may have happened tonight."

She closes her eyes and pinches her nose. "Halloween," she mutters under her breath. "I'm scared to ask, but what kind of stuff."

"My ex-girlfriend's tongue disappeared."

"I was not expecting that one. I need clarification. Were any animals harmed tonight?"

I shake my head. "Not unless you count my ex-girlfriend, but it's a long story."

"Give me the *CliffsNotes* version."

I sigh and look around to make sure nobody is listening. No chance of that. The band is playing, and I have to strain to hear Lily Jane when she speaks. She leans her ear toward me so she can hear better. "My ex-girlfriend was talking shit to Eliza and me. She wouldn't shut up. Then, her tongue wasn't there, and it was like she swallowed it. Eliza ran away. I ran after her. Eliza told me she wished Millie, that's my ex, would shut up. She blamed herself for making Millie's tongue go away. We went to Eliza's and searched for a four-hundred-year-old book that was kind of scary, made a potion in her kitchen that had to have hair added to it, and went to the dog park to respect the moon. Millie got her tongue back, but dog hair got in the potion. Now, every dog in town is howling and barking like they've gone insane. Eliza ran away. I ran after her, but I lost her in the woods," I say, taking a deep breath when I'm finished. "That's pretty much it."

Lily Jane runs her hands through her hair. "This is terrible. I finally got her out of the house on Halloween, and now this."

"Did you know magic is real?"

"Of course, I know magic is real. My best friend is a witch."

"How silly of me. Anyway, do you know where she would go? Is there a place that upset witches go when they have a bad date?"

"Starbucks?" she shrugs.

"She doesn't have a secret hiding place with a big cauldron or something? She doesn't like to dance naked in a rock circle at the edge of town when she's upset?"

Lily Jane scrunches her nose and taps her foot against the stage, adjusting the gold cord at her waist while she thinks. "There's a barn that she likes going to that's about a quarter mile from her house. She used to ride horses there when she was young. She once told me she still goes there to think. Did she run through the woods behind her house?"

"Yes!"

"That's probably where she is, but we should get a group of people to help find her. You check the barn. I'll go to her house and wait to see if she comes back," she directs, taking my phone from my pants pocket and entering her phone number into my phone. "Here's my number if you find her. Do you know anyone that can help us search?"

Paul is in no shape to find his ass with both hands, and Millie can't be trusted. "No. We should have people check the woods. She could have fallen or be hurt and need help."

"Good thinking," Lily Jane nods, adjusting her ponytail.

"Who can we get to help? I moved here a few years ago, but never really got to know many people. I guess I could call a couple of coworkers I have beers with, but I don't have a lot of friends I can call at ten at night to help me search for a girl in the woods."

Lily Jane looks around the crowd like she's

searching for friends. The band stops playing and announces they're taking a break as the crowd moans in protest. Looking around, the crowd is sweaty, and ties are loosened. Women are flushed and have taken their shoes off to dance, and nearby tables are filled with shot glasses and beer bottles the catering staff can't remove fast enough.

Lily Jane steps to the microphone and taps it twice to get the crowd's attention. "Hi. Are you having a good time?" she yells into the microphone with a smile.

"Yes!" the crowd roars back, fists in the air.

"While the band is taking a break, we can play a game. Would you like to play?" The crowd roars again, and I cover my ears from the loud whistles. "My friend Eliza is missing. Who here knows Eliza?" she asks, raising her hand.

Most of the crowd raises their hand, and I'm reminded that it's a small town. Not everyone who raises their hand is Eliza's age, and I can't imagine she is friends with all these people, but people know *of* her. Maybe they knew her mother. Some people groan and roll their eyes, and I remember Eliza saying that the town wasn't always nice to her.

"See this guy back here?" she says, and the crowd cranes their necks to see me. I wave back. "This is Eliza's raffle date for the evening. Eliza was in the common ground woods behind the dog park, and we haven't heard from her. She may be hurt. We need a few people to come with us and look. Do we have any volunteers?"

"Why can't the police do it?" someone shouts.

Lily Jane looks back at me. "Should we call the police?" she whispers.

I shrug. "I think she has to be missing for twenty-four hours before they do anything."

Lily Jane turns to face the crowd again. "She has to be missing for a day before they'll help. Can someone help us?"

People mumble, shrug, and look at each other, but nobody raises their hands or offers to help Lily Jane. Some men laugh with each other and make motions like their grabbing boobs. Christ, what has Eliza endured in this damn town?

Desperate, I walk to the microphone and nudge Lily Jane over so that I can speak. "Excuse me," I say, getting the crowd's attention. "My name is Jake Salt."

The crowd stares at me, not at all impressed by my name, and I clear my throat. "I work for the post office, so some of you may have seen me around town. More importantly, I really like Eliza Owl."

The mumbling in the crowd quiets, and women bring their hands to their chests, covering their hearts at the romantic gesture of a man admitting

TORI ROSS

that in front of an entire charity event.

One man that's laughing with his friends raises his hand. "Why do you like her, man? You need to run far away from that one before she turns you into a toad."

"I first saw Eliza when I delivered her mail a year ago," I say, ignoring him. "You may think that I fell in love with her looks, but I didn't. Someone called on the phone while I was there, and it was her voice that did it for me," I sigh, remembering the soft voice she used when she answered the phone. "I've never heard such a kind voice before. It made every nerve ending on my body jump to attention, and I wanted to talk to her. I just never did because I'm a huge pussy."

"Aww," a woman in the front row says.

"I finally got a chance to talk to her in person tonight. I could never work up the nerve before, and that's on me. But she talked to me first tonight. Guess what I found out?" I ask, looking at the ceiling and running my hands through my hair. "I learned that she's more than a pretty face and a sexy, kind voice. She's smart, and I learned she cares about this town so much that she spends Halloween away from all of you because she's convinced she may hurt someone. I'm sure we've all heard the rumors about her witch powers."

"Where have you been, dumbass?" one man calls out.

I clear my throat and answer. "I just moved here a few years ago. I'm not local."

"All the shit is true, mate!" a man yells from the back with cupped hands. "I lit one of her candles, and I didn't need hair plugs."

I nod and clap. "Congratulations on avoiding male baldness. See! She cares about your hair happiness," I add, pointing in his direction. "However, I learned that there is something special about Eliza. I didn't believe, but I do now," I mumble into the microphone and shake my head. "I won a date with her in the raffle, and it made my night. Then, she got upset by something. It wasn't me, but I went after her. I couldn't find her, but now I'm worried she's hurt or scared. Please," I beg, slapping my hand to my chest. "If you've ever liked someone so much that your toes curl when they walk into a room and knew right from the start that that person was your person, help me. Help me find the woman I want to get to know even better. Help me make sure she's safe."

Lily Jane sniffles next to me, and her lip trembles. "You really like her, don't you?"

"I've never wanted to get to know someone better like this in my entire life. I just want a chance with her, Lily Jane."

I turn to the microphone again. "If that doesn't convince you, then step outside. You'll hear dogs barking and howling. Every dog in town is going nuts. We need Eliza to fix it, because only Eliza has the power to do that."

People turn their head in the direction of the doors like they can hear what I'm talking about, even though I know they can't. They look at each other and shrug, checking phones to see if there's anything on the news about crazy dogs.

"Help me find her. We all need her."

"This sounds like an adventure!" a drunk man in the front row yells. "I'm in. What are you thinking, man?"

I scratch my head and think for a moment. "Well, Lily Jane is going to check her house to see if she ends up back there. I'm going to check an old barn she likes. The rest of us should split into two groups. We need to check the woods," I say, the crowd nodding along.

"We're not exactly dressed for a rural search and rescue," one woman says, pointing to her Catwoman outfit.

I look around a moment. "Anyone that has an outfit that's not conducive to the woods can search Main Street. Maybe she's at one of the places in town having a cocoa. Anyone dressed like a farmer, and there seems to be a lot of us, can search the woods."

A few other rumbles come from the crowd. Hands raise, some excitedly, others slowly. People nudge their dates, questioning if they want to go look for Eliza. Their dates shrug and smile in return. Nods and "OK" or "Sure, why not?" ripple through the crowd.

Lily Jane smiles next to me and pats my shoulder. "Way to go, Jake. Let's go get our girl."

CHAPTER 9

Eliza

This place used to be beautiful, and I came here every day after school to see the horses. The farmer sold the horses a few years back, then died, leaving the barn in disrepair. Long grass and overgrown weeds surround the faded red building and grow as high as the first story windows. The gravel road up to the door is spotted with weeds, and deep ruts in need of a gravel fill trip me as I run to the dirty white door and fling it open.

The smell of horses hits my nose, even after all these years. Used condoms and beer cans litter the entry way area, signs of teenagers using this for a party and an illicit sex spot. As I walk further away from the door, the litter decreases, the darkness of the back part of the barn only for the bravest of teenagers or those exploring on a dare.

I swing open the door to one of the back stalls, and the hinges creek, sending a flock of pigeons flying from the upper rafters and startling me. Hay bales sit in the corner, and I run my hand over one, checking for rubbers and shattered beer bottles before I sit down. The bales are surprisingly clean, given the decrepit state of the rest of the barn.

I curl into a ball, my knees to my chest and my skirt up to my waist. I don't care if someone walks in and sees my underwear. I duck my head into my thighs and let the tears flow.

Tears for disappointing this entire town yet again. Tears that I left Mom's book in the basement without being in a plastic bag. Tears that I fucked up the best blind date I've ever had. He was a gift from the universe, landing right in my lap, and I scared him away. I would have had to, right? No man in his right mind would want a witch that boils fish, removes people's tongues, and makes dogs bark uncontrollably.

Having Jake disappointed in me is bad enough. But the whole town is going to be angry as fuck when they figure out what I did to their dogs. Howls and barks from the town still reach my ears out here, a quarter mile away, and I cover my ears as tears fall off my chin.

I cry for what feels like hours until another sound reaches my ears. My name and other shouts come from a distance, but I can't tell if they're yelling my name in anger or laughing at me.

Lifting myself onto the hay bale, I rub the window glass, which only moves the grime around in a smudged circle on the pane. I squint through the dirty window and immediately slouch back down, almost falling off the bale in my

TORI ROSS

haste to get out of sight.

My nightmare is happening. Townspeople. A lot of them. And they're all dressed like farmers and holding torches. Well, they're holding their phones as flashlights, but nobody uses torches in this day and age. I didn't see any pitchforks, but who knows what weapons they brought with them.

They're hunting me.

I run my hands through my hair and pull on it when I reach the end. This is how I'm going to go out, huh? It's just like the stories my mom told me of my ancestors. You piss the town off, and they come for you. I glance out the side of the window and see the willow trees around me. Am I going to hang from one of them in just a few minutes? Will they take me back to the bonfire and burn me? Will I even get a trial? A chance to explain myself? Surely, we've progressed as a society since the hangings and drownings of my female line.

But have we really?

I search my dress pockets for my phone before I remember that I left it at my house on the kitchen counter. Thoughts of not being able to say goodbye to Lily Jane brings a fresh round of tears, and I close the horse stall before pushing the tiny metal latch into position. It feels flimsy in my hand, the tiny piece of metal the only thing between me and an angry mob.

Shouts come closer, and the main door to the barn opens as I silently back up against the hay bale and slouch down like a cornered rat. Heavy footsteps stomp through the barn, and a cell phone light swivels across the ceiling, sweeping left to right as the person comes down the row of horse stalls. The person opens stall doors one by one up the row, and pigeons and starlings scatter with each stall opened.

"Eliza? Are you in here?" a familiar voice asks. "It's Jake. If you're in here, let me know you're safe."

I'm tempted to answer him and tell him I'm safe. But I don't dare. Is he with the angry mob outside? Has he decided I need to be run out of town for my accidental dog incident? Is he mad about me running from him in the woods.

I scooch back further in the corner of the stall. It's better and safer for him if he doesn't find me.

His steps stop outside the stall door where I'm hiding, and he tries the door, finding it locked. "Eliza?" he whispers. "Are you in there?"

The flimsy lock holds, and I stay silent, biting my lip so hard that I taste blood. Every nerve in my body wants to yell for him and talk to him about this entire night. I want to hear what he thinks of me no matter how bad it may be.

A tear slides down my cheek, and my nose starts to run. I involuntarily sniffle, then cover my nose. Shit!

"Are you crying?" Jake asks in a kind voice that breaks me. "Please let me in, Eliza."

"I'll just hurt you," I mumble back.

"You won't," he soothes, running his fingers down the stall door. "You couldn't hurt anyone."

"I hurt Millie, and I hurt those dogs."

"I wouldn't say excessive barking is hurting them, Eliza. You have to open the door so we can fix it."

"I'm scared."

"Of what?" he asks.

"Of you judging me. I'm scared that I disappointed the one guy that I didn't want to disappoint." I walk over to the stall and lean my forward against the door. A tear trickles down from my eye and lands on the hay under me. "You're the first guy I've talked to in a long time, and I wanted to impress you. Not hurt your ex-girlfriend, freak you out with the witch thing, and turn all the dogs in town into raging lunatics."

"Will you open the door so I can see you?"

"Are you here to hurt me?" I ask.

"What? No! Why would you even think that?" he asks, his voice husky with hurt that I'd think he'd hurt me.

I swing the stall door open and wipe my nose on my sleeve. Jake's hair is rumpled with no hat in sight, and he leans against the stall doorway with such masculine ease that I want to run my hands up his chest. How did I miss him around town? He's gorgeous, and my lips tingle at the idea of kissing him again.

He pushes off the doorframe and comes to me, pressing his forehead against mine. "Do you know how long I've waited for this, Eliza? How long I've waited to kiss you like we started to earlier tonight?"

"Why didn't you talk to me?"

"I was scared of rejection. I worked through how I would talk to you a million times. I dialed the numbers to your shop more than I can count, hanging up before I entered the last one. What would I have said? That I delivered mail to you once and thought you were gorgeous? You would have thought me a crazy stalker. Do you think I'm going to let some barking dogs and a couple of date mishaps ruin this night?"

"What about Millie?"

"To hell with Millie. She's fine. It's you I'm worried about."

"Am I going to be burned in the bonfire?"

He backs up and wrinkles his brow. "What the hell are you talking about? Nobody wants to do that to you. Well," he says, waffling his head back and forth. "Millie may want to do that, but she'd have to get through me and the entire town. They really don't hate you as much as you think."

"Bullshit!"

"True," he counters, reaching out for me and putting his palm on my cheek. I lean my head into his warm hand. "I hear you even cure baldness."

He plants a soft kiss on my forehead and pulls me in for a hug, and I sway at the proximity of him. He makes my legs weak whenever he touches me, and my hands tremble as they run up his jacket.

He notices and pulls back. "Let's sit down, and you can tell me why you ran away," he says, leading me to the hay bale.

"I already told you. I really shit the bed with Millie's potion."

"You cured her. So, there was a little bit of an unintended consequence. We'll cure that, too. It wasn't anything you did. It's really windy out there, and the breeze probably blew dog hair around, some of it flying into the potion. Personally, I think it's funny as fuck that you made my ex-girlfriend drink dog hair."

He pulls me to his side, and I lean my head against his shoulder, breathing in his scent. It's masculine with a woodsy shaving cream smell. I close my eyes and let the strength of his biceps surround me, keeping me safe as I hide in a horse stall.

He tilts my chin up with one finger. "She's not around to throw a purse at me. Do you want to pick up where we started earlier?" he asks, and I feel his smirk on my cheek along with his warm, mint-scented breath.

Uncontrollable lust moves through me. It's been longer than I'd like to admit since I've enjoyed the company of a man, and I'd very much like his company. I pull him down until he's on top of me on the hay bale. Stalks chafe against my arms and tangle my hair as I settle into the bale, Jake stroking my hair and planting sweet kisses on my lips. He rubs his nose against mine before moving his lips to my jaw, up to my ear, then down to my neck. I tilt my head back and wind my hands in his hair.

"Are you sure that this isn't an elaborate ruse to get me to come out of the barn and face the mob of townspeople?"

"I will never hurt you, Eliza," he says, dragging his hand up my hip.

Jake moves his mouth back to my jaw, trailing kisses up the side of my face and moving to my earlobe. He caresses my hair back from my face, and the pads of his fingers are gentle on my scalp. His breath is heavy and tickles my skin as his warm mouth trails every inch of my face, neck, and shoulders. I wrap my arms around him, pulling his warm body closer to me as the hay scratches the backs of my arms and legs. He notices and pulls back, taking his jacket off and placing it on a spot next to me. "Slide over," he whispers. "I don't want you to get scratches."

"Such a gentleman," I mumble, pulling him back to me and running my hands up his chest. His pectorals are tight, and his heart pounds under my hand. "Why would I get scratches?"

"I plan on being in here for a bit," he laughs.

I'm thankful I'm lying down. I wouldn't be able to kiss him without swooning if I was standing. "What would you like to do?" I ask, blood rushing to body parts I haven't used in so long that I forgot they work.

I hook my leg around him, and he gives me a light kiss on my lips before moving up my jaw again.

He nuzzles my ear and kisses it lightly. "Well, if you're down for it, I'd like to give you at least two orgasms, and it may cause thrashing and writhing in pleasure. That hay could really cause some problems."

"Are we about to have the stereotypical roll in the hay?" I chuckle against his neck. The shaving cream smell is stronger at his throat, and I close my eyes to savor it.

"If that's how you'd like to spend the next few minutes, sure." His hands reach under my skirt, and he hooks his fingers in my black, lacy panties. "Can I take these off?"

"Please," I beg, my voice a husky whimper as I unbutton his shirt and slide my hands against his tight, hot skin.

He pulls my panties off and lays them on the hay next to us. "Can this skirt come up further, too?" he whispers, bending down and planting a kiss on my knee.

"You can do anything you want, Jake."

"Anything?" he says, cocking an eyebrow. "What an interesting offer."

I moan as his soft lips move to my thighs. "At this point, I'd even be down for that burning at the stake thing if it means you give me those two orgasms you promised."

He laughs into my skin, and I run my hands through his hair, attempting to nudge his face higher. He takes his time, and it's downright maddening. He kisses up my thighs as my hands paw at his hair, and his kisses leave a wet trail up my legs.

Just as he's about to reach my slit, he pulls back, and I whine, fisting the back of his shirt at the neck. "Don't stop."

"I want to draw this out and drive you crazy, Eliza," he whispers, pushing my dress higher and kissing my abdomen.

"Just unzip me, for fuck's sake," I say, sitting up and pointing to my zipper at the back of my dress with shaking hands.

He reaches around me, his eyes never leaving mine, and drags the zipper down the back of my dress. Pulling it down, he kisses as he goes, dropping soft pecks on the top of my breasts, down my stomach and on top of my mound. I hiss as his kiss lingers there, and I settle back against the hay with my legs wide open for him.

I've never been so brazen. At least, not that I can remember, and I'd think I'd remember lying spread eagle on a hay bale in an old barn, begging a man to devour me. I beg with my eyes, my whimpers, and my hand stroking his face. The world could explode right now, and I'd only be disappointed that I wouldn't get to have his mouth on me.

"I love seeing you open like this for me," he murmurs, kissing the top of my slit and dipping his head lower.

I whine and fist his hair as he drags his tongue from my pussy to my clit in one long, leisurely lick like he's savoring an ice cream cone. He mumbles something about waiting so long to taste me, but the words don't make sense in my head. They're like puzzle pieces, and my brain only registers that there's a hot man's mouth on my clit, licking and sucking like he's never had such a delicious meal. "Jake," I whisper, bucking into his face.

My whispers and little moans make him more exuberant. His tongue moves to my pussy, and he dips it inside of me. He moans before kissing the skin around my clit and moves to flicking his tongue over me with firmer pressure. Fuck, he's good at this. Some guys only focus on the clit or a hole. With Jake, every single inch of my lady bit area is getting attention.

Waves of pleasure move up and down my body, the hay digging into my back forgotten. He groans as he sucks on my clit and pushes his face deeper into me without holding back. I'll take whatever he gives me. My core and thigh muscles tighten, and my ass comes off the warm jacket under my buttocks. "Fuck, Jake. Don't stop," I moan, pulling his hair.

He slides a hand up to my stomach, rubbing and stroking my skin. I grasp his hand, and he joins my fingers with his, holding my hand as I break apart on his tongue.

He was right when he said there would be squirming and writhing. The trembling seems to last for minutes, but I've lost track of all time and space. When my eyes flutter open, I'm surprised to find myself in a horse stall.

"One down," he mutters, kissing the wetness from the inside of my thighs. His face is wet with my want, and I pull him up to me by his hair.

"I want you, Jake. I want to make you feel as good

as you made me feel."

CHAPTER 10

Jake

Oh, shit. Oh, shit. Oh, shit.

I just ate out Eliza Owl, and she wants to make me feel as good as I just made her feel. From the way she rode my face, I'm not sure that's possible, but my dick is at attention and willing to give it a try. Her taste has maddened me to the point that I can't think of anything else going on in the world besides the fact that I selfishly want to intimately know every inch of her body.

I've waited so long for this woman, and I've thought about the possibility of this moment more than I'd like to admit over more than a few showers. But I'm going to make her beg for me. I need to hear her beg for this, if only to fluff my own ego.

Her eyes lock with mine as I move up her body, kissing her belly, running my tongue up her hips, and moving her bra aside to lick her nipples. Her body tastes earthy and of something primitive with a hint of salty sweat.

I kiss her mouth, letting the taste of her own

desire transfer to her tongue. "You taste so fucking good, Eliza. What do you want?"

She laughs. "I think I've had enough already. It's your turn."

"No, ma'am. I promised you two orgasms, and I'm going to deliver or die trying. Do you want this?" I ask, sliding a finger inside of her warmth.

Her body is tight, and her mouth opens as her eyes flutter at my finger. "Or maybe two?" I whisper, sliding another finger in to join the first one. I make a come-hither motion with my digits, and she whimpers. "Are you going to whine for me, Eliza? Are you going to cry out for me when I make you come again? It's just you, me, and a bunch of pigeons in this barn. Moan all you want. The birds won't tell anyone."

I thumb her clit in gentle strokes, and her warm hand covers mine, moving it across her as she rocks into my thumb. "Jake," she whispers as she pushes me back a little, her hands coming to my pants and unbuttoning them.

Before she pulls them down, she runs her hands over my cock and inhales sharply. "I knew it was huge."

"Is that what you want? Or do you want me to keep my fingers where they are, Eliza?" I coo, fisting her hair with my other hand, forcing her to look at me to tell me what she wants.

"I want this," she says with a shaky voice, running her fingers over my cock.

"As you wish," I say, kissing the tip of her nose.

I remove my fingers from her and lick them once while looking her in the eyes. Her hand slides down my chest and stomach, and she removes the final buttons of my shirt, flicking the fabric aside and running her fingers through the lines of my abdominal muscles.

I work my pants and underwear down to my knees, and she hisses when she sees my cock in the moonlight coming through the window. She runs a tentative hand up and down my shaft, and I inhale at her touch. "Eliza," I whisper, gritting my teeth and rolling my neck.

I reach for my wallet in the back of my pants and make short work of rifling through it for the condom that's probably been in there too long. I squint and hold it up to the window, looking for the expiration date. "Is it expired?" she whines under me, practically panting. "Please say it isn't expired."

"It says to use by November 2022. We made it with one day to spare," I say, holding up the condom like a prize. "Actually, one hour to spare."

She giggles and brings her hand to her own sex, rubbing her clit as I open the wrapper and roll the condom over my length. I'm desperate to be inside of her, connected to her body, but I hesitate and slide my cock where her fingers linger. "Allow me," I say, rubbing my dick over the bundle of nerves I mouthed mere minutes ago.

My fingers and her hand have already done the work, and it takes only ten seconds of rubbing my throbbing, hard dick over her until her back arches again, and she grips my hips. "Jake, fuck!" she moans. "Fuck me!"

"Beg. I want to hear you beg, Eliza."

"Please, Jake. Please. I want this so bad. I need this. I want to make you come so fucking hard."

I slide into her, her body still shaking from the orgasm, and she wraps her legs around my waist. Hay digs into my knees, but I don't care. I'm inside of her like I've fantasized. She's wet, and she's tight as fuck as I thrust into her and bury my face into her neck.

"Eliza," I whisper, my senses overwhelmed.

The taste of her is still on my tongue, the smell of her vanilla body wash is in my nose, and the heat of her body is wrapped around me. Her nipples slide against my chest as I push into her over and over, and they tighten into pointed peaks from the friction. The tightness clenched around my cock is the crowning jewel of all sensations, and I close my eyes to savor her. "So beautiful," I mutter into her skin.

"Does it feel good, Jake?" she asks.

"You have no idea how good you feel, baby," I coo. "I could fuck you all night. Maybe I'll take you home and do that. Would you like that?"

She moans under me, and I rear back onto my knees, throwing one of her legs over my shoulder to push deeper into her. "Is this OK? I don't want to hurt you."

"I like it when it's hard, and it's good when it hurts a little," she coos back at me. "That just means that I'll feel you tomorrow."

Her face flushes, and she props herself on her elbows, her head thrown back as I ride her hard. I run my hands down her breasts, and they jiggle in rhythm to my thrusts. I press my hand to her stomach, holding her steady as she shakes and wriggles around me.

"Eliza," I moan as the familiar pleasure stirs in my balls. They tighten, and electric pleasure moves from the tip of my cock, up my back, and causes electric pings in the base of my neck. "Fuck, baby. You're driving me insane."

"Let go for me," she whispers, covering my hand at her stomach.

I throw my head back and follow her direction to let go. I thrust hard into her, and she tightens her leg around my waist. She reaches down and grabs my ass, pulling me into her even harder. "That's it, Jake. Fuck, yes."

Her eyes squeeze shut, but I can't take my eyes off her. I want to drown in how gorgeous her body looks in the moonlight. I want to commit her to memory just in case this never happens again. I'll do anything to make it happen again, though. I want this woman over and over in every position, begging for me, whining, and panting as I take her. I'm desperate to please her more than I care about pleasing myself. I'd love to stay in this musty barn and bend her over the horse trough. I know we have to fix the town dogs, but I selfishly want this woman all to myself.

My dream girl. The one I've wanted for so long.

My orgasm comes hard, and I bite my lip as I push into her one last time, grunting her name. Hot spurts fill the condom, and she pulls my ass into her as deep as I can go as my dick twitches with release inside of her.

Sweat dribbles down my temple and dots my chest. She wipes the chest sweat away with her hands, flexing her fingers like they're thirsty for me.

Once every drop of come is wrung from my body, I settle on top of her. I stroke her hair, wet at the roots with her own sweat and kiss her softly on the lips. "I hope you know I want to do that again," I whisper.

"Same here. I haven't had sex in so long," she says, her voice husky and shaking.

Her leg muscles tremble around me. The increasing wind howls against the windows as we kiss softly. I tell her how beautiful she is, how she is the best I've ever felt around me, and how lucky I was to have her raffle ticket in my pocket.

She runs her fingers up my back in leisurely strokes. "I'm so glad I met you, Jake. It's like you're a Halloween miracle," she whispers. "It's been so long since I've met someone that overlooks the weird magic stuff." She squints and purses her lips. "Now that I mention it, I've never met someone that overlooks the weird magic stuff. It's kind of why I'm single."

I stroke her hair and nuzzle her nose with my own, my satisfied cock still inside her, and I'm hesitant to break our connection in fear I won't have it again. "I don't care about that," I whisper. "That's just a cool little perk, as far as I'm concerned."

"Cool little perk?" she laughs. "After the mess I've made tonight?"

"Let's talk about that for a minute," I say, pulling out of her with a sigh. "How can we fix it? Tell me how I can help, and I'll help you. So will Lily Jane. Hell, the whole town is ready to help you."

She tilts her head and squints her eyes. "They are? Aren't they hunting me to hang me from the nearest tree?"

A laugh bubbles up from my chest. "Wait! Is that

what you think is happening?"

"They're all dressed like farmers and waving flashlights. It's the modern equivalent of torches and pitchforks."

I look behind her and shake my head. "I keep fucking this up and making it look like your entire night is a stereotypical Salem witch hunt," I chuckle. "I'm so sorry, Eliza, but they aren't hunting you. Lily Jane and I gave the town this amazing motivational speech about how wonderful you are and how much I like you. We thought you were hurt or scared in the woods. Lily Jane told me about the barn, and I told the volunteers I would check here. That reminds me. I need to text Lily Jane and tell her I found you."

"She's probably worried sick," Eliza groans, slapping her hand to her forehead.

"Yeah, um," I cringe. "We got a little carried away, huh?"

She pulls me closer to her again, wrapping her beautiful legs around me, and I run my hands up her hips. "If I tell her we got carried away in the barn, she'll forgive us. She knows it's been a long time for me."

"Back to the town situation, you know they came out to try to find you because they were worried."

She rubs her face and looks at the ceiling. "You

understand why it's hard for me to believe that, right?"

"I get it," I say, stroking her hand. I can't keep my fingers out of it. "I know that witches haven't been historically revered. But times have changed."

"They haven't. The things I hear would curl your toes. I hear a lot of people ask 'Why are we celebrating witches?' especially during Halloween. People still throw out that *don't suffer a witch to live* malarky."

"That's what it is, Eliza. There will always be close-minded people. The world is changing, though. Sure, it doesn't seem like it at times. But the people that don't care about you being a witch far outnumber the nutjobs. In fact, that's why the nutty people are becoming so loud. They're losing their grip on the world that they've enjoyed for centuries. They're afraid. You said it yourself tonight," I say, kissing her cheek. "They hate what they fear, and they fear education, acceptance of ideas not their own, and people not relying on ancient direction to make decisions."

She nods, and a tear trickles down her temple. I quickly wipe it away for her and kiss the wet spot it left. "No crying, Eliza. I won't let anyone hurt you. Ever."

She buries her face in my neck. "I just wish I could fix the dogs."

"What would your mom have done?"

She sighs and sniffles. "She'd make a potion or whip up a spell if there wasn't already one in the grimoire. She was strong at spells and potions."

"What is your witch strength?" I ask.

"Witch strength?" she chuckles.

"On TV, each witch has a special strength or power. Something that they excel at. What's yours?"

Her eyes flick to the barn rafters above us. "I guess I've never really thought about it. Mom was always good at potions, so I tried to be good at it, too. It didn't work out well."

"Maybe that's the problem. Your strength may be something completely different from your mother's specialty. When something has gone really well, what was it? What did you do that worked?"

"I've just said a few blessing spells under my breath as I melt hot wax to make my store's candles."

I stare at her forehead while I think. "Heat. You're using heat at all of those times, right? You also boiled the fish at that coy pond."

"I thought you said it was a filter malfunction," she grins.

"That was before I saw you actually use magic and before you just told me your specialty is melting wax and burning things while you do spells. You must be gifted in working with hot things. Fire. Flame. Smoke. Things like that. If you play to your strengths, I bet we can fix this."

I roll to my side, and I instantly miss the heat of her body. I need to let her up and try to fix this, though. I find my pants on the barn floor and slide into them before handing her the panties on the hay next to us. I fire off a quick text to Lily Jane that Eliza's OK, and my phone pings back a thumbs up emoji a few seconds later.

We dress in silence, and I give her time to think about what to do. Distant sounds of dogs reach my ears when I stand next to the window, and I check my watch. It's after eleven, and the town will grow more irritated with the barking every minute it goes on.

I button the last button on my shirt and throw my jacket over my arm, ready to put it around her if she's cold. "What's the plan, Eliza?"

She stands up, adjusts her dress, and takes a deep breath. "The only thing I can think of is grabbing the grimoire and getting to my candles. If you're right about heat being my strength, I need to get to my shop."

CHAPTER 11

Eliza

Jake's hair is a rumpled mess, and I steal glances at him out of the corner of my eye as he sits on my counter, calmly kicking his legs like a child. Behind me, Lily Jane rummages through the shop and flicks a red dusting cloth over the display tables. "Can you stop that?" I ask, my voice shaky. "I don't need dust flying around while I'm trying to work. Lord knows that I could cause a huge dust storm or dust tornado. That would be my luck tonight."

"I don't know," Lily Jane smirks, walking to me and picking a stray piece of hay from my hair. "From the look of your hair and Jake's hair, I'd say your luck is working just fine tonight."

Heat moves up my body, and Jake grins as he runs his hand up the back of his neck. I can still smell him on my skin, and I'm sure I reek of old hay and sex. It's hard to believe that I was losing my shit under him half an hour ago. Memories of the most amazing sex I've ever had flood my brain every time I look at him or hear his voice, and I need to focus on the grimoire in front of me.

"Besides, I can't sit around the shop and listen to you read an old book," Lily Jane adds.

"Then, why'd you come? You left your own event."

"This is more important. I wanted to support you. Besides, the silent auction and raffle are over. The band is playing. People are drunk and happy, and the town knows you were found. There's no use me being there until cleanup time."

Jake runs his hand down my arm, and I shudder. "You have to stop touching me. I can't concentrate because I want to take you in the back room," I whisper.

"Sorry," he grunts in a husky voice that goes straight to my nipples. I roll my neck and try concentrating on something besides the mental image of him bending me over my backroom counter and taking me from behind.

I flip through the pages of the grimoire, looking for a blessing or spell to protect animals or calm animals. "Can't you just do a reversal spell or something?" Lily Jane whispers.

"I can't do that," I huff, annoyed that I can't just look through the book in peace. "If I do that, Millie may lose her tongue again. This needs to be a new spell to calm animals or generally calm the town. Will you let me work?"

She holds up her hands and backs away, leaning

on a display table and making a buttoning motion on her lips.

My mother's grimoire doesn't have a table of contents or chapters on certain topics. That happens when you have several generations of witches contribute to a book over the course of four hundred years. Loose papers come out in my hand as I turn pages, and I stick them back where I find them. The photos and illustrations are faded, and I squint to make out old-time cursive writing that looks nothing like the cursive I was taught in grade school. Even if I never add my own spells or potions to the book, I make a mental note to catalog the book and add an index for future generations of witches. That can be my service to this book.

Eventually, I find a spell that may work. "Here we go," I murmur.

"You found something?" Jake asks, sliding off the counter and putting his hand on the small of my back. I instantly feel protected and supported. I can do this.

"This is an old one, and I hope I'm reading it correctly," I say, tapping my index finger on the page. "It's a spell calling for gentle demeanor. It's the closest I can find. It looks like it was used in the old days to control husbands with anger issues or mean dogs."

"The dogs aren't mean. They're just barking,"

Jake says.

"It should still work and calm them down if I put the intention there."

"How old is it?" he asks.

"Well, I can tell it was written before the nineteenth century started. Does that make you feel better or worse?"

"Better, actually," he says and shrugs.

"Really?"

"The really old witches knew what they were doing, right?"

I nod and hope I can read it correctly. Some of it's rubbed out, and we can't afford another fuckup tonight. If this doesn't work, we're absolutely screwed because I'm out of options.

"What ingredients do you need?" Lily Jane asks behind me. "I can help."

"I have everything in the duffle bag," I say, nodding to the bag we brought to my shop that contains my mother's pantry items. "I have snail shell, pondweed, and nettle. This should do it. Jake, hand me my mortar and pestle under the counter there," I say, pointing to my grinding pot.

He grabs it and sets it in front of me. "Lily Jane, grind this snail shell for me."

Power moves through my veins as my confidence builds. I have a recipe to follow, I have my best friend next to me, and I have the sexiest man I've ever met looking at me like I'm a goddess of wisdom and witchcraft. Electricity practically flies out of my fingertips as I gather a glass for the candle and white wax sticks. Is this what it's like to have control? I felt the power move through my body earlier tonight, but I couldn't get it to fully release. This time, I feel it move out of me and into the air like a thin layer, surrounding my body and making my skin tingle. The air practically crackles with it. I've never felt it like this before, and I take deep breaths to pull the power back into my body. It's like a cycle; push it out and breathe it back in.

This feels new. Sure, I've felt power move through my body, but I've always dialed it back. I even tempered it with Millie's potion earlier tonight, worried and expecting that something would go wrong. I've pushed my power down out of fear of messing up. Is Jake right? Have I had this power all along but just needed to find my strength? Have I just needed to allow my natural love of candles and flames flow through me?

I close my eyes and say a silent prayer to my mother, wherever she is. She would want me to nail this. All of the women of my line would want me to get this right. I can practically feel their eyes on me as I heat the wax and mix minced pondweed and crushed nettle together, combining it with the decimated snail shell that Lily Jane hands me.

"Stay quiet," I direct. "I'm about to put some

serious intention into this."

Both Lily Jane and Jake nod, and I meet Jake's eyes. They're bright and smiling, if it's possible to smile with eyes. They're crinkled at the corners, and I inhale sharply. He believes in me, and for the first time in a long time, I believe in myself.

I lean over the bowl of crushed ingredients and pour the melted wax into it. I grab a spoon from my duffle bag and gently stir the mixture, closing my eyes and mumbling a blessing under my breath. It's nothing special. I can't think of a cutesy rhyme about happy dogs or calming animals. I just push my love of animals and good thoughts into the universe, repeating the words under my breath like the Catholics of my town say the rosary.

Steam reaches my face as I stir, the wax turning the murky green color of the pondweed. It's a putrid color, and it smells like dirt. I can't sell this one in my shop, that's for sure.

It'll get the job done, though.

I know it will stop the barking dogs like I know the back of my hand.

I roll my neck and stir the wax a few more times before pouring the contents of the bowl into a glass candle holder. The liquid practically shimmers as it settles to the edges and top of the glass. "We just need to let it set for a few minutes," I whisper.

Jake and Lily Jane don't answer, taking my direction for silence seriously. I bend down and put the candle in the mini refrigerator under the counter. I use it when I need candles to set quickly. I shut the door, and Lily Jane looks at me with wide eyes. "You can talk now."

"Oh, thank God," Lily Janes exhales. "Do you know how hard it is for me to be quiet?"

"I do," I nod. "It needs to set for a couple of minutes before I burn it. That should do the job. Fingers crossed. Distract me while we wait."

"How?" Lily Jane asks.

"I don't know. Talk to me about a mundane topic."

She smiles an evil smile. "Sure. Let's chat about why you have hay in your hair and why Jake looks so happy and relaxed, shall we?"

"Talk to me about anything but that."

"Oh, no. You both need to spill. On the first date? In an abandoned barn? Eliza Owl, I'm shocked at you."

"Have you seen him?" I ask her, waving at Jake and referencing his hotness like he's not standing two feet from me.

"I have, and I totally think you should run away and get married this second. However, as much as I approve of this young man, this is uncharacteristically fast for you."

"I like him," I shrug and look at him out of the corner of my eye. He's smiling, and the dimple is out.

"I like her, too," he says in a quiet voice.

He reaches out and grabs my hand, stroking his thumb over my index finger. "Thanks for talking to me tonight."

"Thanks for having the match to my raffle ticket," I smile back. "I got lucky when we were matched."

Lily Jane clears her throat and points at her ear. "I think I deserve a 'Thank you, Lily Jane, for dragging my butt to the charity auction and making me join the raffle where I met an awesome guy.'"

"Thank you, Lily Jane," I giggle, bending down to check on the candle.

As soon as I open the door, the dirt smell hits my nose. "This one's going to stink when I burn it, so you may want to step back," I say, setting the candle on the counter. It's no longer steamy, and the top of the wax is set enough to burn.

"Here goes nothing," I say under my breath.

"Should we be quiet again?" Jake whispers.

I nod. "Better safe than sorry," I reply, flicking the lighter in my hand and feeling the heat.

Something is wrong, and my hand hovers above

the candle wick, not ready to light it. There's something off about the lighter in my hand.

It isn't natural, and I feel the disconnection to fire in my hand. It's like using a wiffle ball bat to play professional baseball. My other hand itches, rubbing my fingertips together to create fiction. My fingers want something.

I set the lighter on the counter, and Jake squints and shakes his head. I step back from the counter and take deep breaths. My mother did this, and I know I can, too.

I touch my fingertip to the candle wick as Jake and Lily Jane both gasp. My finger doesn't erupt in flame, and I don't shoot fireballs out of my fingers. I breathe out, a belly breath as my mother called it. It's like the breaths I blow out before an orgasm, and I clench my core muscles. Heat flows through my body, my arm, and down to my hand.

The heat that leaves my fingers is so intense that the wick starts to smoke like an extinguished match.

I breathe out again and push all my intention into my hand, creating heat that would burn non-witch hands as blue flame appears like an aura around my hand.

The blue surprises me, and I tilt my head, making a "huh" sound. Part of me expected my hand fire to be orange or red like normal fire. Instead, it looks like a gas stove's flame or pilot light. Out of the corner of my eye, Lily Jane's mouth and eyes are wide open. Jake grips the counter with white knuckles, mesmerized by my hand.

I tap the blue aura to the wick, and the candle makes a popping sound like crackling paper, before a yellow light appears on the wick, and a steady flame settles onto the wax.

"I did it," I whisper. "I made fire. Just like Mom," I say, turning to Jake with tears in my eyes. Will he run away? This is where men run screaming from the lady that can make fire with her hands. He steps toward me, his eyes focused on my own as he pulls me into his arms, tilting my chin up to him. "You aren't going to run away?" I ask.

"I'm here, and I'm not running. I also believe in magic now. That was no slide of hand bullshit from a magic show," he says, bringing his lips down to mine.

His tongue seeks my own and enters my mouth in gentle strokes. There's no rush or senseless passion like in the barn. This is reverence. Respect. My knees immediately go weak, and butterflies fly in my stomach.

I wrap my arms around him and pull him closer to me, stroking the back of his neck. I can't get enough of him tonight, and I marvel that I found him. The cliché thought of wondering where he's been all my life runs through my head.

Lily Jane clears her throat, and we break our deep kiss, his lips glistening a couple of inches from mine. He breathes deeply as we stand forehead to forehead for a minute as Lily Jane huffs and opens the door to my shop, the bell above the door tinkling with the movement and strong wind outside.

"I think it worked, Eliza."

"What worked?" I ask, inhaling the smell of Jake's skin that now includes a slight hay smell.

"The dog candle," she drawls. "You know...what we came here for."

"Right!" I say, pushing myself back from Jake and clapping my hands. "I almost forgot."

"I bet, you dirty whore," she laughs.

I walk over to the door, Jake hot on my heels, and stick my head out of the doorway. I look left and right up the street, not stepping over my shop's threshold for fear of being arrested for disturbing the peace.

Nothing. Not a sound.

Wind rustles fallen brown and orange leaves up the street, and the streetlights cast a yellow glow over the sidewalk. The sign above the coffee house next door swings with the breeze, and a plastic bag dances in the air above the flower shop across the street. A stray black cat I feed every morning crosses the street and meows, hoping for an early can of tuna or saucer of milk. A sudden gust of wind knocks over a nearby trashcan, but the street is otherwise silent.

"I did it," I say, tears forming and threatening to run down my face.

"Of course, you did," Jake says, his strong hand on my back. "Now, let's go celebrate with the entire town!"

CHAPTER 12

Jake

"Are you insane?" Eliza asks, backing away from me. "You two are one thing. Going back to that party after I thought the town was going to hang me for making every dog in town go nuts is something quite different. Tell him, Lily Jane. Tell him how the town has tormented me my entire life."

"Eliza," I say, stepping to her. She won't get away from me so easy. I can't let her go, and I can't let her think this town hates her enough to punish her. "They don't all hate you. That whole group was out searching for you to make sure you were safe. They weren't going to hang you. They had confidence in your ability to fix it. Guess what?" I ask, waving my hand in the direction of the still burning candle on Eliza's shop counter. "You did fix it."

"He's right," Lily Jane says, and I nod in appreciation of her support. "When Jake talked to the town, they believed in your powers. Sure, there were a few assholes. Always have been. But they were willing to help look for you. You need to suck it the fuck up and go back to that party. You need to tell them what you did to fix the dogs and the truth about what you are. It's time to set the rumors straight."

"No!" Eliza grunts, walking to the candle and blowing it out. Smoke swirls from the wick, and the putrid smell of crushed snail shell and pondweed fills the area around the counter. "I can't talk to them."

"Do you think it's better that they come up with their own rumors and legends?" I ask. "Because they already have. Aren't you tired of them getting it wrong? Aren't you tired of the few assholes being able to bully you about it? Own that shit, Eliza! Be proud of it. I'm proud of you, and I've only known you for a few hours."

"Jake's right. Witches have cowered in fear for centuries. Your ancestors had to hide in the shadows," Lily Jane says, thumping her palm on the grimoire. "Every woman that wrote in this book was scared for her life and practiced her magic in darkness. Even your mother didn't flash her shit all over town. There was a hushed up, word-of-mouth pipeline telling other women about her power. But you can be the one that comes out of the darkness, Eliza. You're the one that can do good things for this town and tell the world that witches have been persecuted enough for the ages."

"I'm scared of how much some of them hate me.

I don't feel safe. I never have."

"They are few and far between, making a big noise because they know their numbers are dwindling. Fuck them."

Eliza works her lip and wrings her hands like she's thinking about it. Lily Jane and I look at each other and shrug as Eliza cleans up the candle work area, neatly stacking her mortar and pestle with others on the shelf and wiping the counter with a white rag. She wipes her nose and looks at the grimoire, putting her hand on top of it like she's asking her ancestors their opinion.

Eliza finally nods and slides her hand into mine. "Will you stand next to me in case somebody comes for me?"

"Nobody will attack you, Eliza, but I'm here."

"Let's get it over with. Can you drive?"

I pull my car into the same spot it was parked before, and we get out of the convertible, shutting the doors quietly like we're afraid to make noise. It's not like that matters. The band's music blares from the building into the still-full parking lot. It doesn't look like anyone has left the party yet, and a few cars with Uber stickers on the back are idling in front of the building.

"Looks like the party is getting pretty wild. Maybe I should have charged more for drinks," Lily

Jane says, cracking her knuckles. "I hope I get my event rental deposit back."

We walk to the doors and fling them open. Nobody notices Lily Jane walk in, but people stand aside with open mouths as Eliza walks through the crowd, my hand on her back. Her steps are heavy, and she takes deep breaths. My hand pushing her through the crowd is the only thing that keeps her moving.

"You're here!" several people say as we pass them. Some yell, "You found her!"

Eliza ducks her head like she's shy, and I put my arm around her as we approach the bar. "Can I get you a drink?" I ask. "You look like you could use a stiff one."

"I already had a stiff one tonight, but a glass of wine would be nice," she says, her lips curling into a smile.

"I'm glad you still have your sense of humor," I chuckle. I kiss her on her temple and nod at the bartender. "One white wine and one whiskey."

I need a hard drink. Beer will not come close to soothing the night I've had. This has been one for the ages.

Eliza leans into me, and I suddenly want to skip her coming out at this party. I want to take her home and have my way with her in a proper bed without hay scratching our backs.

The bartender puts our drinks in front of us, and we turn away from the bar only to see the entire town stealing looks at Eliza. They talk to their friends in hushed tones and nod in our direction, looking Eliza up and down. Women with coy smiles look at me like they've just noticed that I exist, even though I've lived here for years. Sure, the ladies on my route have noticed me, but I don't get out much. They look at me because of my proximity to Eliza. Do they think I'm a witch, wizard, or whatever the male equivalent is?

"I told you this was a bad idea," Eliza mumbles, sipping her wine.

"They're just fascinated," I say, even though some of the looks she gets are clearly unwelcome glares.

She tightens the grip around her wine glass and focuses on me, taking deep breaths as Lily Jane climbs the stairs to the stage again and taps the microphone. The band takes their guitars off their shoulders, like they're taking another break, and shrugs as they walk off stage.

"Let's hear it for The Grinders!" Lily Jane claps, referencing the band leaving the stage. The crowd screams and whistles.

They've definitely had too much to drink.

Lily Jane leans into the microphone. "As many of you may have seen, we found our girl," she says, gesturing to Eliza. Every head in the place turns to stare. "Thanks to all of you that searched for her. We're glad she's..."

A man approaches Lily Jane and bends down to whisper something into her ear. She covers the microphone with her hand and cocks her head to the side. I can't read lips, but the man's face is furrowed, and he runs a hand down his beard scruff. He shakes his head and shrugs as Lily Jane blows out a breath and puts her hands on her hips.

The man walks off, and someone from the crowd raises their hand. "Are they kicking us out of here? The party's just getting going."

"Nothing like that," Lily Jane says, waving her hands in a downward motion. "We just seem to be having some trouble getting the bonfire started. The wind is too fierce. It keeps blowing the fire out."

Boos fill the room, and the crowd lifts their drinks, scowls on their faces. Middle fingers go up in the air. Lily Jane waves her hands, trying to quiet the crowd again, but the crowd is angry it won't get to top off the night with the bonfire.

Lily Jane's lip trembles, and her eyes dart around the room, looking for help. Her eyes meet Eliza's, and Eliza stiffens at my side. "Eliza! Come up here," Lily Jane beckons.

Eliza shakes her head and makes a throat cutting gesture. Her body trembles under my hand at her back.

"No, come up here. You fixed the dogs. You can fix this, too. You can light the bonfire."

The crowd quiets as suddenly as they were riled. Heads swivel between Lily Jane and Eliza, as if the town understands that Eliza can boost a crappy libido, but they're unsure if she can make fire. People smirk, laugh, and shake their heads with doubt.

Too bad I've seen her do it.

Eliza doesn't take the stage, and Lily Jane doesn't get her to go up and talk to the town. Muttering moves through the crowd, and several men point in the direction of the back field as dread moves down my spine. Whatever they're planning, I don't like it. People nod and scowl at Eliza.

A few men walk toward Eliza and me, and I move to stand in front of her, setting my glass down on a nearby table. Even though I'm between them, several men pat my back and push me out of the way as they pick Eliza up and put her on their shoulders.

I tussle with a man twice my size until I eventually duck under his arm, scurrying after the men carrying Eliza. "Eliza!" I scream, but she can't hear me over the sound of the crowd.

The entire building cheers and pumps their fists in the air. "Shit!" Lily Jane says into the microphone, covering her hand with it before giving up and joining the crowd. She runs down the stage steps and fights her way through the crowd as I do, pushing people aside and hoping they don't get trampled.

"Get her, Jake!" Lily Jane yells, sandwiched between two men dressed as Ghostbusters.

The men carry Eliza toward the door like she's the winning quarterback and chant, "Fire starter!" the entire way out of the door.

Everyone follows. Even the band shrugs and walks after the crowd, gently leaning their instruments against their amplifiers. Caterers and bartenders, Paul included, leave their stations and follow the crowd with curiosity, and wait staff members drop their trays on the nearest table without a care.

The crowd jostles me around, but I push my way through. "Eliza!" I yell, reaching up toward her when I'm about ten feet away from her outstretched fingers. "Eliza, I'm here."

"Am I the starter?" she yells, twisting around on the shoulders carrying her. "Am I starting the fire, or are they going to use me like a human Duraflame log?"

I shake my head and reach for her, but the crowd is too thick and loud. They chant, hoot, and holler. Lily Jane catches up to me and grabs onto the back of my shirt so we won't get separated, and we push our way through the crowd to get to Eliza.

Eliza's visually shaken. Her lips tremble, and her eyes are swollen. "Put her down!" I yell, finally catching up to one of the men holding her. Hot rage moves up my back, and I clench my fists. I grab the back of the man's neck, pulling him to the ground as Eliza slides toward the grass with him. Lily Jane catches her around the waist and pushes a guy that reaches to pick Eliza up again.

"What are you thinking? Can't you see you're scaring her?" I yell, shaking one man and grabbing the other by the shoulder. One of the men pushes back, and I don't think before slamming my fist into his nose.

Blood spurts onto the other man's face, and a hush moves over the crowd as I shake off the pain in my hand and knuckles. The men carrying Eliza back up like they just realized where they are, the punch to their friend's face like a glass of cold water being thrown on the group.

Both men back away from me, one wiping his face, and the town surrounds us. Men look at me with thunderous anger, and adrenaline pulses through me before seeing Eliza. She's looking around with big eyes and in a crouch. Leaning over and ignoring everyone, even the dicks that look like they'd fight me, I rub Eliza's back as she squats on the ground. "It's OK, Eliza. I'm here. They have to get through me first."

"What were you thinking?" Lily Jane yells at the

town, turning in a circle. "Did you think carrying the town witch to a fire pit was a good idea? Look at how scared she is!"

"You said she could light the fire," one man says. His eyes are glassy, and he slurs his words.

"You're drunk as shit and not thinking straight," I say, putting my arm around Eliza's waist and standing her up. "Do you have any idea how scared she is because you all hate her?"

This silences the crowd, and a couple men close to me scratch their heads. "Why would she think that?"

"I don't know?" I ask in a mocking voice. "Maybe because you've bullied her, pranked her, called her names, and told her she was going to hell for her entire life. Maybe because her ancestors were burned at stakes and drowned. You seriously thought carrying a witch to a bonfire and chanting that she was the fire starter would calm her?"

"Oh," a woman drawls, chewing on a drink straw. "We didn't think about that."

"No, you didn't think. None of you did," I say, hands on hips and turning in the circle. "Do you know what this woman has been through tonight? Does anyone notice that the dogs are no longer going nuts?"

People stop to listen, and nothing but wind rustling the trees reaches our ears. People in the crowd blush or bite their lips, looking away from Eliza.

"This woman helped my ex-girlfriend tonight," I say, gesturing at Millie. She stands next to Paul with a blank look on her face, but she nods when I mention her. "Listen to that! My date for the night helped my ex-girlfriend after my ex was mean to her. You all have been mean to her for her entire life, and she still helps you. She quieted the dogs. She makes candles that cure your baldness or help you get laid. And this is how you treat her? You all should be ashamed of yourselves for your behavior tonight. In fact, you should be ashamed of how you've treated her and her mother your entire lives.

"I've only known her for one night, and I know that not one person in this town deserves this woman," I say, catching Lily Jane's eye. "Except you, Lily Jane," I whisper.

Lily Jane waves me off and makes a rolling motion with her finger. She's fine with me scolding the town. Her encouragement emboldens me further. I'm ready to fight anyone that comes near Eliza. She won't be hurt by this town a moment longer. If she's ever threatened again, I'll throw her over my shoulder, sell my house, and take her somewhere far away from this place where she can't be hurt.

"Eliza should leave this town that's treated her

like shit for years. You don't realize how great you have it. She's fun, kind, smart, and she has feelings, you know? She hurt when you thought it was funny to hurl rocks at her house when she was young. She hurts now when you tell her she's going to hell. But you can't see anything past your own noses and your own beliefs. You haven't shown her an ounce of empathy her entire life except when you want something. You're all selfish assholes! Unless she does something to help solve one of your urgent issues, you don't care how people treat her."

The town stares at me in silence. Behind me, Eliza brushes dead leaves from her skirt and squares her shoulders back. Her chin rises, and her fists clench. Even Lily Jane backs away from her, brow furrowed by Eliza's sudden confidence.

Eliza takes a deep breath through her nose and blows it out. Her chest heaves, but she puts her hand over her sternum like she's trying to calm her breath and pounding heart. She looks at me, and I don't talk further. It's not my talk to have. I may protect her, but she's going to handle this once and for all.

I take a step back and nod, signaling to her that I have her back in whatever comes out of her mouth.

"I'm sorry that I'm not the witch my mother was, and I'm sorry I haven't been here for this town before. I hid away for a long time because of how I was treated. But I'm here now, dammit!" she says, pointing her finger in the air. I flinch a little and back up another step. So does the crowd. I know what that finger can do, and the crowd is shocked by Eliza's sudden wrath.

"No more!" Eliza says, pounding her fist into her palm. "I will not hide any longer! I will not cower from people that seek to hurt me while ignoring people I can help. I will not hide my power, and I will use it to help each and every one of you. If you're sick, I'll do my best to make you better. If your cat is lost, I'll get it home. But God damn all of you if you think less of me because of who I am!"

My mouth won't work. It's full of cotton, and I'm not sure where to place my emotions. Should I clap? I'm not sure if she's done. Her eyes meet mine, and she smirks. It's a smirk of power and confidence, and it's the first time I've seen it on her mouth.

"We love you," a woman says, and every head swivels to her. The woman is in her early twenties and sporting a mohawk. Glitter dots her cheek, and sweat has caused her extensive makeup to run, but she smiles at Eliza like she's greeting an old friend. "I'm sure some people in town are scared of you, but I'm not."

"I bought one of your candles when my boyfriend died," a mousy woman with round glasses says. "I didn't know where to turn, and the candle was labeled as providing comfort. I tried it, and it comforted me whenever I burned it. I should have thanked you for that, and I never did. I guess I was scared. Thank you, Eliza."

Yet another woman raises her hand. This woman is one of the oldest here, maybe late thirties or early forties, and looks like a mother on her first wild night in years. "I'm not scared either, Eliza," she says. "Good for you for being who you were born to be. I'm sorry if you ever received a sour look from me."

Another woman with purple hair raises a fist, "Fuck those old ass witch hunters!"

Other women nod and smile at Eliza. I hear, "We trust you, Eliza!" and "We'll never let anyone run you out of town." Women throw their arms over the shoulders of the other woman next to them, grit their teeth, and nod at Eliza, yelling words of encouragement and whistling.

A tear runs down Eliza's face as she looks at the women cheering for her. The men mostly remain quiet, backing away a little as if noticing that this conversation isn't about them. It's about women being misunderstood and judged for centuries, even by each other, and finally coming together to say enough.

Eliza meets my eyes again, and I nod. "Do your thing, sweetheart" I murmur, raising a fist with the town women. "Show them what a badass you are."

She comes to me and plants a kiss on my lips as the entire town, men and women, cheer and throw up their hands. Lily Jane puts her fingers in her mouth and whistles. Out of the corner of my eye, I even see Millie slow clap with Paul next to her, ogling her breasts.

Without a word, Eliza turns away from me and the town and walks to the bonfire pit with a presidential walk that reeks of confidence. Wood is stacked into a perfect teepee shape so the air can move under the wood to fan the flames. The smell of lighter fluid fills my nose as we follow Eliza.

She stops at the base of the firewood and looks up at the sky. "I got this, Mom. I'm not fucking hiding any longer, and I won't let anyone else hide either," she says in a whisper. I only hear it because I'm right behind her.

She flexes her fingers and rolls her neck before pointing her index finger at the wood. The dreaded witch's point, denigrated for centuries as the cause of all evil.

She smiles and inhales. As she breathes out, the blue aura appears around her hand as if the breath is pushing the fire from her finger. The entire town, except for Lily Jane and me, gasps in awe. Muttering waves through the crowd as people adjust to seeing a blue flame around the town witch's hand.

Not one person in this town will dare fuck with her again.

She gently touches her glowing finger to the wood, and it catches the dry kindling covered in lighter fluid. Once an orange flame ignites on the wood with a crackling sound, she moves to another area a few feet away and touches her finger to a different piece of wood.

We watch, open-mouthed, as Eliza walks around the bonfire circle and lights small fires every few feet.

Despite the breeze, a couple of flames sheltered by other wood catch and combine to light up the sky as the crowd cheers, chanting Eliza's name.

CHAPTER 13

Eliza

Jake's soothing hands massage my scalp, still picking stray hay out of my hair and setting it on the side of my bathtub. "We really rolled around in that hay, huh?" he whispers, placing a kiss on my wet neck as shampoo drips down my back.

I bring my hand up to his face, running my fingers over his wet skin. "It's been a hell of a night, huh?"

"It's not night now. What is it? Three in the morning?"

"You were the one that thought we should cap the night off with a long bath," I gesture to the bubbles covering my breasts and the fake tea light candles that line the tub rim. I didn't want to use real candles in case we got them wet or knocked them over if we got too exuberant. "I would have been content to curl up under a blanket."

"We both stunk to high heaven."

He grabs my shower sprayer we pulled down and rinses my hair, finger combing it as the suds run into my jacuzzi tub. The jets beat against my feet, and I relax into the safety of his firm chest.

After the fire started, the party moved to the bonfire. People sang, the band brought their instruments out to the field, and the crowd drank until the police showed up and made everyone leave. Well-wishers surrounded me, shaking my hands and patting me on the shoulders all night. Some women hugged me and apologized for ostracizing me all my life. Men fist bumped me, congratulating me for making fire with my fingers.

He was with me the whole time. Jake stood behind me, his hand on my back, and it felt like it belongs there. I know he stood next to me to protect me, worried someone would try to hurt the witch that can make fire.

I'm exhausted. I've made two separate potions, started two fires, come clean to the entire town, and met a guy so wonderful that I'm still not sure he's real. That doesn't even include amazing barn sex and making his ex-girlfriend's tongue disappear and reappear.

He saw me falling over with exhaustion and suggested taking me home. Once here, the stink of bonfire and old hay was too much for both of us, and he ran me a bath, complete with bubbles, and brought me a last glass of wine for the night.

I sip the wine as his hands move through my hair, up and down my arms, and he wraps his strong arms around my breasts. He hums a little as he nuzzles my ear. "I want more of this."

I smile into my wine glass. "More of what part?" I'm unsure if he's talking about sex or spending time together in the future.

I get my answer when he slides his hand through the bubbles to my slit. "Let's start with more of this?"

"Aren't you tired?" I ask, my eyes closing as familiar pleasure of his circling finger moves through my body.

He moves his hand away, and I immediately catch it, sliding it back to my clit. "Exhausted," he breathes into my ear. "But if it means I can enjoy this one more time tonight, I'll sleep when I'm dead."

I slide around to face him, the water sloshing over the tub and splashing into the tea lights. I straddle his lap, and bubbles slide down my body. He wipes bubbles from the tips of my nipples, and I lean forward so that our foreheads press together. "You were my hero tonight," I whisper.

"I helped, but you were your own hero, Eliza," he says, moving his thumb back to my clit.

I push my face into his shoulder, breathing the familiar smell of my bubble bath and the smell of what I'm learning is just his smell. He grabs my hips with his hand that isn't at my clit and slides me so that his erect dick is at my entrance.

I take the lead and slide onto him, impaling myself onto his cock and kissing his shoulder. "God damn," he whines next to me. "Do I need another condom? Should we get out?"

"I have an IUD," I mutter, my voice already husky as I start to rock against him.

The jets stop blowing water, and I reach behind Jake to hit the button on the wall next to the tub. As I lean up, he catches one of my breasts with his mouth, sucking and flicking his tongue over my nipple at the same time.

My hands wind through his hair as I rock and writhe on him. I feel full when he's inside of me, like finding something you lost. I just didn't know I'd lost him because I just now found him.

I'll be damned if I'm without this man tomorrow.

His thumb at my clit, his dick inside me, and his mouth on my nipple combine into an unholy trinity of pleasure, and my body tightens in response. I rock faster against him, chasing my third orgasm for the night as he pants under me. "Take it, Eliza. Take what's yours, baby," he urges, noticing my body's response around his cock. "I want to feel you come undone."

His cooing and encouragement push me over the edge, and I throw my head back, whimpering as my body trembles and my belly curls. "Good girl," he whispers under me.

He runs his hands up and down my back, and I roll my neck, enjoying the feel of his finger massage on my skin. He roams everywhere. My hips. My thighs. My pelvis. My breasts. His hands eventually settle on my throat, and I throw my head back, rocking into his dick and his strong hand.

My wet hair whispers across my back, and my eyes flutter as his thrusts increase, pounding into me from below. The water moves in rhythm with us, sloshing over the faucet and over the edge. Fear of the mess or the water dripping down into the kitchen below briefly enters my mind, but it's pushed aside by the pleasure of him. He moans and pants as he fucks me, and his pleasure is more important to me than the reality of later cleanup.

Water drips from his earlobes and his shoulders, running down in lines down his chiseled chest as I reach for his body. I want to explore him the way he explores me. I want to know what every inch of his body feels like. I want to feel how every muscle flexes, and what his face looks like before he comes.

He grips my hips harder, pulling me into him so hard that I gasp. He leans his head back against the white tiles behind him, and a wet lock of hair flops onto his face. I immediately smooth it back and run my hand down his cheek, feeling the new stubble on his skin. "Come on, Jake. Let me hear you let go with me."

He bites his lip as I brace myself on the tile behind him so I can meet his thrusts and push against him. His thighs tremble under me, and his shoulders tense. "That's it. Fuck me, Eliza. Fuck the shit out of me."

I do as he asks, rocking against him. I grip his hair and force him to look at me. "Open your eyes, Jake."

"I can't. You feel too good," he replies, licking his lips.

"I want to know what your eyes look like when you orgasm."

He forces his eyes open, and I push my forehead to his again. As soon as our skin connects, his eyes darken into black pools, and he struggles to keep his eyes open. His own stomach tenses, and he moans my name one last time before stilling inside of me, his chest heaving as he breathes through his nose.

"Good boy," I coo, giving him one small peck on the tip of his nose.

He smiles, and his head lolls to the side of my tub. "Now I'm definitely exhausted. Sleep next?"

I slide off of him with a groan from both of us and turn off the tub jets. His hands slide down my body like he's loathed to let me leave the tub, but I step out of the tub onto the bathmat, water dripping down my body. I reach for my robe and wrap it around me before getting a towel for Jake. Grabbing his hand, I help pull his dripping body up from the tub.

"Come sleep next to me," I say, my voice more begging than directing.

He steps onto the bathmat, dries his body in seconds, and runs a hand through his hair. I turn and walk to my adjoining bedroom, and he follows behind me in silence. He throws the wet towel back into the bathroom as I grab a t-shirt and panties from my drawer, and he slides his boxer briefs back onto his body.

Silently, we crawl under the covers of my bed and curl into each other. The pink sheets are cool to the touch, and the downy white blanket is warm. There's no discussion on whether he should stay the night, and there're no words of having to be at work early the next day for a meeting or making excuses to leave. I pull him closer to me, my hand resting on his thigh. He kisses my forehead and inhales the scent of my shampoo.

The way his body fits against mine is comforting. I don't think I've ever felt this kind of connection, and I don't want him to leave.

CHAPTER 14

Jake

She looks so still and peaceful when she's asleep. No worries about her power. No fear of being ostracized by the town. Just deep breaths as her chest moves up and down under my arm around her rib cage. I prop myself on my elbow and stare at her, mesmerized that I'm in her bed.

If you had told me twenty-four hours ago that I'd be in her bed and watching a line of drool darken her pink pillowcase, I'd have called you a liar. My hands tentatively reach out and tuck a stray hair behind her ear, only to have it slide right back to where it was. Even her hair won't be controlled.

Last night was weird, terrifying, and all-around heaven. I woke up an hour ago, worried it was a crazy dream and that I imagined the barn and the bathtub, but it's true. I've spent the last hour decompressing, coming to terms with a world where magic exists and trying not to wake her. My fingers itch to stroke her hair, rub her back or drag themselves lazily up her arm. I don't want to be creepy, though. It's our first morning together, and I'm not sure of her personal rules on touching while she sleeps.

Eventually, she stirs, and her eyes flutter open. "Jake?" she asks, her voice husky from disuse. "Are you real? Was it all real?" she asks with a small smile.

I chuckle and kiss her forehead. "All real. I thought the same thing when I woke up. I'm glad I stayed last night or else I'd be very confused right now."

She snakes her arm under my own, pulling me close to her. "I have morning breath," I say, tilting my head up so it's not directly on her nose.

"No, you don't," she says, touching her finger to my lips and mumbling under her breath. Warmth enters my mouth, and a peppermint taste burns my tongue so much that I bite it and breathe out.

"Did you just mint me?"

"Did it work?"

"You've seriously never tried that before? Dear, Lord, I'm not a guinea pig," I laugh into her neck. "You could have boiled me."

"I'll do it to myself if it makes you feel better," she whispers, pursing her lips. "Happy now?" she asks, blowing minty breath into my nose.

"Immensely. Happy All Saints' Day, by the way. Want to celebrate the holy day?"

She laughs and pulls my lips to hers. Our kiss is

soft and leisurely with no rush or expectation for the kiss to move to sex. My hand rubs the fabric of the old concert t-shirt she wore to bed, and I flick the elastic on her black panties.

Our mouths move together in rhythm, and her tongue explores my mouth, flicking against the tip of my own. We kiss for minutes as she runs her hands through my hair.

She pulls back and rubs the tip of her nose against my cheek. "I hate to break this up, but I need to open the shop," she says with a sigh. "I'm not sure how busy the shop will be, but my witch sense tells me people may be interested in my candles today. In fact, this may be a turning point for my business with the townsfolk."

"I need to get up, too. I have to be at work at eleven."

She reaches for her phone to check the time. "I have a little time before opening. Want to have breakfast first? I have eggs."

"I'll do you one better," I say, kissing her on the forehead one last time and rolling away from her. My body instantly misses the heat of her skin, and I feel cold. Lonely. I swing my legs out of bed and reach for my pants, the bonfire smell and dried whiskey on them filling my nose. "You get ready for work. I'll cook."

This isn't just eggs," Eliza says, walking into the

kitchen. "It smells amazing in here."

"Yeah, I found biscuits in the fridge." I place jelly and butter on her snack bar and scoop large spoonfuls of scrambled eggs on a plate. Scooting the platter toward her, I put my hand over hers. "I hope scrambled is OK."

"As long as it comes with coffee, I don't give a shit."

I pour her a mug of coffee and watch the thick, black liquid settle before handing it to her.

"What happens now?" I ask, leaning against the granite countertop.

"I drink it."

"No," I laugh. "Can I see you again?"

A dark cloud passes over her face, and my stomach drops. "Are you sure you want that? I mean...now we're in the morning light, do you still want to take on being involved with a witch?"

I scowl, and my heart speeds up in my chest. I can't lose her the morning after. No way. Not after all we went through last night. We bonded, right? This wasn't just one night. It can't be. I may have only known her for one evening, but I can't imagine not having her next to me.

I clear my voice and roll my neck as she sits calmly in front of me, buttering a biscuit. "Do you have any idea how long I've wanted to talk to you? Do you think making fire with your hands is going to scare me away?"

"I hoped it wouldn't, but you wouldn't believe the number of one-night stands that run as fast as they can as soon as something happens that they deem weird."

I back away from the counter. "How many one-night stands are we talking about?"

She giggles and waves her hand in front of her face.

"Do you want to see me again, Eliza?" I ask, my heart in my throat. This is the moment of truth. This is when I know if this will work. Because I'll make it work if it's the last thing I do. God dammit, I'll make it work every day of my life if she's willing to give us a chance at a relationship.

She sighs and looks at the refrigerator behind me, her mouth formed into a frown. Tears burn in my eyelids, but I don't blink. I won't let them out of my eyes.

"It would be a waste," she whispers, looking back at her plate.

"What would be a waste? Us dating? You know you're good enough, Eliza. You're amazing, and..."

"No, Jake," she says, holding up her hand and tilting her head to the side. Her eyes sparkle like a child's when they've been naughty and got away with it. "It would be a waste of that spell I put on the raffle ticket table to pair us if we didn't try to date."

Her words rattle around in my brain for a moment, like a puzzle cube that someone's shaken or thrown in the air, the pieces falling where they want. I pinch my nose and take deep breaths to clear my mind. Eventually, the puzzle pieces click.

"You paired us?" I ask.

"I may have said a little spell in my head and wiggled my finger. If you think I was going to take a chance that you ended up with Millie, you're crazy. I wanted you as my date from the moment I saw you in that ridiculous witch hunter costume."

"Pilgrim costume."

"Sure, Jake," she grins.

I sip my coffee and study my jelly-covered biscuit for a moment, pushing it around on my plate. "I thought your magic doesn't work for your own benefit."

"It doesn't. I cast the spell that you'd be paired with Millie, and I'd be paired with Paul. Think about it, Jake. What are the actual chances of Millie getting you and me getting Paul out of a hundred raffle tickets? I guess that even the universe knew it wasn't to my benefit to date Paul. I took a gamble that you'd make a different decision, and you did.

"It was you who switched the tickets. That was lucky, too. As you know, my magic is unpredictable at best on Halloween. I just pushed it out and told myself that if the results are different, I'd live with it."

"You sly little witch."

"The thing I'm most amazed by is that I did it without heat, candles, fire, or my mother's grimoire. It's like the universe gave me a push in the right direction. I guess I saw you and had more intention in my spell than I thought at the time."

"Maybe you should write in your grimoire how you did it. Your daughter or granddaughter may need to know such things someday."

"I've never been confident enough to write in it," she shrugs and sips her coffee.

"You should," I say. "I think you've earned your place in the family line last night. If nothing else, you earned some street cred when you stood up to the town and did magic in front of them without fear. That's something no other witch has done."

"Do I really want my daughter or granddaughter manipulating who they spend time with? I was wrong to do it. Like I said, I'm lucky it didn't backfire."

"How would it backfire? Do you think you'd be eating breakfast with Paul right now?"

She laughs. "He wouldn't have made it that far."

"Good, because he only knows how to make toaster pastries for breakfast," I laugh, biting into my biscuit.

"Thanks for picking me, Jake," she whispers, her eyes meeting mine.

"How did you really know I'd switch the tickets?" I ask.

She sets her fork down and swallows her last bite of eggs. She smiles, but only one side of her mouth moves, making her grin look sinister. "I only suspected. But I told you, Jake. An Owl woman just makes stuff happen on Halloween."

EPILOGUE

Eliza

"Are you ready?" Jake asks, straightening his witch hunter costume.

We got him a real one this year. Well, we pieced together a long, black leather jacket, knee high boots, and a length of chain wrapped around his shoulders. It goes well with my witch costume the town expects me to wear tonight. It's the same costume as last year, and I sigh that this will probably be my standard costume going forward.

I rub my hands over my tulle tutu and practically feel the power vibrating in my hands. This must be what my mother talked about all those times when she said she could feel her power moving through her. Since last year when I started to trust myself and my power, I've been much more successful with control.

My shop business is booming from people coming in for several afflictions, and my candles now have the reputation of fixing anything. Need protection of a child? I have a candle for that. Have you lost a pet? No problem. Summoning spell candles are my specialty, and I can summon anything for you, job promotions and lovers included. I only have the added rule that the love candles can't be used to charm an already married or attached lover. Then again, I may have told a few people that if they lie about that, they'll lose their tongues.

I still can't use my power for my own benefit, but that doesn't mean I don't try. Every night, I light a candle for Jake and me and our relationship. So far, so good on that one.

I don't think it's because I light a candle, though.

Jake's amazing, and we moved in together a few months ago when he finally kicked out Paul. Not that Paul didn't have anywhere to go. Surprisingly, Millie and Paul are a happy couple, at least to the public eye. No telling what goes on in private, but we haven't seen hot sauce stains on Paul's clothes, and he seems happy enough. Then again, he's stoned half the time.

I still haven't admitted to them that I put them together. Well, I put Paul and me together, and Jake switched the tickets. I thank the universe every day that I took a gamble that he'd switch them.

"I'm ready. Do you think they'll still be OK with witches?" I ask, straightening my skirt as Jake kisses me on the cheek. The town has been much more welcoming in the past year, but there are still a few vocal people that think I should be burned and protest my shop on Sunday afternoons, marching in front of my shop with white handmade signs on sticks.

"Why would they change their minds?"

"They've had a year to think about it. You know how it works. What seems fun one day will turn into hatred when one person has a problem with it, or one person questions if it's natural. There's always someone that wants to shit on a witch because they think we're evil. One person says I'm evil, and the rest of the town starts to think it. There are enough protesters to make my business look questionable."

Jake smiles and kisses my forehead in the way he does when I get riled up. It calms me immediately, and I take a deep breath. "Most of the town loves you, Eliza. Everyone that matters, anyway. They respect you like they respected your mom. You've never hurt anyone except for those fish, and you've helped so many people just by being who you are."

He pushes his forehead to mine, and I smell his toothpaste and his familiar spicy scent as I take deep breaths. "I love you, Jake."

"I love you, Eliza," he whispers. "But we need to go, or the entire town will come looking for you with torches again so you can start this damn bonfire."

I laugh and nod as we climb into his convertible. The five-minute ride to the convention center is quiet as we put the top down and enjoy another Halloween with perfect weather. There's no wind tonight, and the moon peeks in and out from behind the clouds like it's playing hide and seek.

Jake pulls over and stops before we enter the parking lot. "What are you doing?"

He jerks his head to the backseat. "Get in your parade spot."

"You can't be serious."

"I'll drive carefully. Go ahead and sit like we did the night we met. I promise that this will be worth it."

"Why?"

"Would you just trust me?"

I kick off my high heels and settle myself onto the back of Jake's car with a sigh. "Hold on," he mutters, letting his foot off the gas and circling to the back of the parking lot at five miles per hour.

As soon as he turns near the back field area of the convention center, cheers erupt, and the local high school marching band starts to play. People line the driveway and clap, holding up pieces of firewood and waving as I go by. "Here, take this," Jake yells over the cheering crowd, handing me a bag of suckers from out from under his seat. "For the kids."

Tears sting my eyes as I laugh and throw the suckers to the children running along with the car into the bonfire area. Jake keeps a steady pace, and thoughts of how much my mother would have loved to see me enjoy Halloween like this overwhelm me. She loved this damn town, and she wanted me to love it and be loved in return.

Before Jake can even stop the car, I reach up and wrap my arms around him from the back, leaning my face into the headrest. "Thank you, Jake. Thank you for making me feel so special."

"Come on, you two," Lily Jane says next to me, opening the driver door as soon as Jake puts the car in park. "We have a bonfire to light."

Jake holds out his hand, helping me from the car and placing one small kiss on my cheek. "Go do your thing, baby," he whispers into my ear.

I grab his hand and bring him with me as I walk to the podium set up by the bonfire. At the front of the small stage is a torch like athletes in the Olympics carry, and I take the time to scowl at it as I pass. The town mayor, Marla Cross, stands at the end of the stage in a black pantsuit and cat ears. "Am I being burned at the stake?" I ask her, smiling at her attempt at wearing a costume with the rest of the town.

She chuckles and shakes her head. We thought you could light that, and then we could use it to light the big bonfire. Besides, everyone knows that if we were going to burn you at the stake, we'd just tie you to a pole in the bonfire."

"Well, that's comforting."

"Never, in the history of witch hunting, has a witch ever been burned after riding in like a hero and passing out suckers to children," Jake says behind me, rubbing my back.

"That we know of, anyway."

Mayor Cross steps to the microphone and taps it three times as the crowd goes silent. "Welcome, to the second annual town Halloween bonfire!" she says to an eruption of applause. She waves her arms for the crowd to quiet and the whistles and hoots to die off. "We're going to let Eliza Owl start the fire for us again this year. Eliza?" she nods at me, and I approach the torch.

I reach out to the pole, and energy flows from my core through my arm and into my hand. "Wait! Stop for a second," Jake yells, and I turn my head. I look around, checking if something's happening or someone is trying to stop the event. My stomach drops in fear that they've changed their minds. After all, there's no wind tonight and no reason they couldn't light this with matches.

"What's wrong?" I ask as the crowd mutters behind me.

"This is all wrong, Eliza."

"What do you mean?"

"There's just," he snaps his fingers and looks off in the distance. "There's something missing."

"Let her light the dang fire!" someone in the crowd yells. The crowd picks up the chant and starts a round of "Light the fire! Light the fire!"

Jake waves his arms, shushing them, and the mayor whispers into his ear. She's not in on whatever Jake's doing.

Jake shakes his head at the mayor, ignoring her before getting down on one knee in front of me. I tilt my head to the side in confusion, and gasps run through the crowd as they realize what's happening before I process it.

"Eliza, I can't let you light the fire without doing this first," he says, opening a box to show a simple square diamond set in a platinum band. "We officially met a year ago tonight, even though I had an unrequited crush on you for a year before you made me spill that drink in my lap. But I have you in my life now, and I can't let you get away. Will you be my wife?"

His face turns up to me, and his boyish smile flashes the cheek dimple I love. Tears sting my eyes, and I wipe the wetness from his own cheeks as he waits for my answer with trembling hands.

There's no question in my heart. I somehow managed to find a protective, loving, and understanding man that's also gorgeous. Part of me wonders if I conjured him, I refuse to be without him.

"Of course, I'll marry you, Jake," I sob into my

hands.

The entire town roars with cheers, and the applause is so loud that I cringe. Jake covers my ears with his hands as he pulls my lips to his. His kiss, once exciting and new, is now as familiar as my own taste and lips.

We kiss for a solid minute as the cheers die down. The mayor clears her throat behind us, and Jake and I break apart, looking around like we forgot where we are. "Congratulations, but I think there's a fire that still needs to be lit," she whispers.

"Right," I say, still flushed.

I hold out my hand, admiring my new ring. Jake puts his hand in my other one, his fingers entwining mine. "You got this, Eliza."

"What if something goes wrong?" I ask out of the corner of my mouth. "You got me all excited. I could boil someone."

Jake looks left and right. "I don't see any fish. Or water, for that matter."

I laugh and touch my hand to the end of the torch, feeling the prickly kindling inside the metal rod. Blowing out a deep breath, I focus my energy from my core, through my arms, and into my hand. I flex my fingers and push love and light out of my hand into the torch as a tiny spark ignites the kindling.

I pull my hand back and bend down to the tiny

blue flame in the kindling. Breathing over it like I'm blowing out birthday candles, I blow gently until it catches, and a ball of orange glows.

The crowd erupts again, and Jake squeezes my hand. "You did it. See? Best witch in town."

Mayor Cross takes the torch to the bonfire area and hands it to one of the utility managers. He places the torch against kindling at the base of the fire pit and walks to another spot a few feet away to do the same thing. Eventually, tiny balls of orange combine to form a big fire.

"How does it feel for a witch to be on the other side of a bonfire two years in a row?" Jake asks, nuzzling my neck.

"I can't believe any of this," I say, tears leaking down my face as I look around at the crowd. Children run around with sparklers, writing their initials in the air, and people gather in groups for pictures in front of the roaring bonfire. The flames light up Jake's face, and he smiles down at me. "A year ago, I was down about myself, my powers, and my love life. Then I met you, Jake."

He kisses me on the tip of my nose. "Maybe Eliza Owl isn't the only one that can make magic happen on Halloween," he says, pushing the bridge of his nose to mine.

THE END

Thanks for reading *Winning the Witch*! I adore my readers, and it would help me so much if you leave a review on Amazon. Reviews are lifeblood to indie authors, and they help other readers find our books.

To subscribe to my newsletter to be the first to learn when I have new release, go to my blog at www.smuttybooklady.com and scroll down or follow me on Facebook or Instagram at @authortoriross. Subscribers to my newsletter and blog also get a heads up when I have freebies on Amazon. Sometimes, I ask my subscribers to help me name characters.

Titles by Tori Ross-

Rocks series:
Cherry Burn
Blue Balls
Pistol Fire
Rocks: The Complete Series

The Traveling Calvert Sisters (Romantic Comedy novellas):
Head Over Heels in Hawaii
Loved in Las Vegas
Christmas on the Cruise Ship – November 2022
Wine on Waiheke – March 2023
Turkey in Tennessee – October 2023

Paranormal Standalone Romance:
Winning the Witch

Full-length Romantic Comedy Standalone:
The Cuffing Season Contract – January 2023

Erotic Romance Standalone:
Disco Bar – May 2023

Standalone Novella:
The Flower Festival Fling - February 2023

Jensen City Heroes (Erotic Superhero Romance):
Arson
Thirst
Darkness
Amp

ABOUT THE AUTHOR

Tori Ross

Tori Ross writes romantic comedy and steamy romance. When she's not writing, she runs a podcast called The Smutty Book Lady and Friends and can be seen reading any genre of books or playing pickleball. She lives with her family and a very high-maintenance dog.

BOOKS BY THIS AUTHOR

Rocks: The Complete Series

Deep in the sticks of Missouri is a bar called Rocks where the bartenders are only similar in the fact that they're all unlucky in love...

Cherry Burn - Dylan Wilcox has been gone from Highlight, Missouri for ten years. Nobody has seen him or even received an email as to his location. Worse, he left his high school girlfriend, Cherry Moss, without saying goodbye when he disappeared. When Dylan shows back up in town, clearly changed in the past ten years, Cherry needs to decide if his story is worth her forgiveness and if she can get over her own demons about him leaving.

Blue Balls - Piper Peck loves her life, her friends, and her job. There's only one problem. The local sheriff, Creed McDuffy, has it in for her over her grandma's old hot tub that's considered an eyesore by county enforcement. Unknown to Piper, Creed has had a crush on her since high school and will do anything to get her to look his way. When Creed goes too far and arrests Piper in a last-ditch effort to get her attention, can he ever grovel enough to get in her good graces?

Pistol Fire - Libby Dean is known for being the town pistol. Brock Carpenter is known for being the town's hero fireman. When a fire at Rocks Tavern throws Libby for a loop, Brock wants to comfort her. Libby's not used to comfort, though, and runs away from any affection as fast as she can. But when Brock needs his own comfort, will Libby put aside her pride and step up?

Each short is 12-14k words. HEA or HFN guaranteed!

The Cuffing Season Contract

Savannah Smart comes back to her hometown, Evergreen Hills, to take over as the head librarian over the local library's youth literacy program. She's determined to finish her degree in library science and enjoy a quiet life as a town librarian. Her mother, however, has other plans for Savannah. When a local bar advertises a cuffing season speed dating event, Savannah's mom signs them both up and convinces her daughter to give it a try.

Wilder Lynx is the local bad boy and determined to remain single forever. He also has a new partner every year for cuffing season and even makes his partner sign a deal saying that their relationship ends after Valentine's Day.

As the couple begins their cuffing season, Wilder's feelings for Savannah grow, and he regrets ever making her sign the contract. He quickly sets out to show her he's worth keeping after their Valentine's Day relationship expiration.

Made in USA - North Chelmsford, MA
1332286_9798848955767
09.13.2022 1723